Back Burning Redux
stories | flash fiction | essays

Sylvia Petter

Interactive Press

First published by IP, 2007
New and Expanded Edition, published by IP, 2024
© Sylvia Petter (text), 2007, 2024

Printed in 11 pt Adobe Caslon Pro on 18 pt Lucida Grande by Konway PrintHouse, Malaysia.

Printed in 16 pt Avenir Book on Caslon Pro 12 pt.

ISBN: 9781922830951 (PB) 9781922830968 (eBook)

A catalogue record for this book is available from the National Library of Australia

Interactive Press

Back Burning Redux

Sylvia Petter was born in Vienna and grew up in Australia. She graduated from the University of New South Wales and studied translation at the University of Vienna. She began writing fiction in the early nineties and was taught by Timothy Findley and Peter Carey through the Humber School for Writers in Toronto. She has been featured at conferences of the Society for the Study of the Short Story in English in New Orleans in 2002 and Alcala de Henares, Spain, in 2004. She was an active member of the Geneva Writers' Group where she participated in workshops with Susan Tiberghien, Isabel Huggan, Thomas E. Kennedy, David Applefield, Peter Ho Davies, and Lee Gutkind.

In 2006, as part of a writers' workshop of the Vienna Poetry Academy, she participated in English in the Wiener Festwochen (Vienna Festival) and the annual 24-hour literary reading, "Rund um die Burg".

She completed her PhD in Creative Writing at the University of NSW in 2009, with the critical part of her thesis concentrating on the stories of Janette Turner Hospital, and the creative Part, a novel, *Ambergris*.

Sylvia recently took early retirement from a policy career with a UN specialised agency in Geneva. She now lives in Sydney again. She has a website at www.sylviapetter.com.

Interactive Press
Brisbane

for Maarit

Acknowledgments

Cover art: *Gerfried Mikusch, www.Mikusch.net*

Author Photos: *Glen Sweeney*

Several stories in this collection, some in earlier versions and one in a German translations, have appeared in the following print, online and broadcast media: *Australian Multicultural Book Review, BBC World Service, Buzzwords Magazine, Conspire, Eclectica, Etcetera, Ex Tempore, Gangway, Intercultural Platform, Offshoots, Southern Ocean Review, The European, The Past Present, The Richmond Review, Woman to Woman* and *World Wide Writers*.

Contents

Back Burning

I'm on a flight from Sydney to London and beneath me a haze veils the Opera House. I've just buried Ralph, my mother's husband.

I move to the vacant seat by the window and think of my husband and daughters in England. I think of another man in my life, of the two men my mother loved.

I'd gone to Sydney for my stepfather's funeral, my head filled with visions of brush fires and burning. The outside of the white bungalow, the house I'd grown up in, had still been the same, just the paint on the guttering had started to peel.

My mother and I were in the lounge and she was swaying gently on the settee. 'He was my big love,' she said. My tears were brimming as I sat down beside her. 'But your father was a good man, too,' she said.

Although he'd been dead ten years, there were still reminders of my father—like the frame on the table in the corner. He had fashioned it from tin to hold the now faded photo of my mother at twenty-five. In it her hair was dark and pulled back with just some tendrils at the white collar of her blouse.

I felt her gaze follow mine to the frame on the table. 'Why didn't you leave Dad?' I said dully. 'If you loved Ralph so?'

'There was you.'

'Then why didn't you let Ralph go?'

She sighed. 'You know what happens when the brush fires come. You can't escape them when the wind hits and the bush starts to burn.'

I moved closer to her, hoping the nearness of my body could replace the arms that no longer could hug her. She stroked my cheek with the back of her hand and passed me a tissue. Then she rubbed her gnarled fingers as if trying to straighten them.

'It's good he went first,' she said.

'Do you mean Dad?'

'Yes. But, perhaps I mean both.'

As the plane sets down in Singapore, the pilot announces it is the time of the Festival of Lights. But I'm in transit and for me there is just time to circle the concourse, stretch my legs.

Passengers board and an Indian woman stops at my row, her seat stub in one hand, in the other a red cotton bag embroidered with mirrors. The thin silk of her sari flutters as she squeezes past me to settle in to the window seat.

I sit down again and smell coriander. A man sits down in the aisle seat. He is in his late forties, maybe younger, or older. I wonder if he is a good man, if he is married. He puts on his earphones. I think of doing the same, but something stops me and I turn my head to the Indian woman. Our eyes meet and I feel I'm in a halfway house going...where?

'My son, he has settled in London,' she tells me. 'He married an English girl. I cannot get used to the cold.'

I nod and turn my head towards the man. I don't want to talk to this woman, don't want to listen. It's the sort of thing my mother would have said. I can imagine her words: 'My daughter has settled in London. She is married.'

I shiver. Getting used to the cold was now my own problem. I think of my mother, of how fragile she looked at the funeral. The Indian woman leans slightly towards me. I glance at her face. A ruby thumb stroke marks her forehead.

'I have two daughters in Singapore,' she says. 'One has her own business. Her name is Neela, she is very successful.' The old woman pauses as if expecting a comment.

I smile politely.

'I tell her success does not always bring happiness,' she continues. 'Neela says she is happy.'

I think why shouldn't she be happy. Then I wonder if the woman will talk all the way and stare past her out the window.

'She is not married,' the woman says and lets the hem of her saffron sari slide through her gnarled fingers. 'The other,' the woman whispers as her eyes warm into amber, 'her name is Sabine. She has made me a grandmother.' She pauses. 'And she has married well.'

The clatter of the stewardess' cart drowns out my wondering whether Sabine, too, had been successful. The man next to me orders a beer. I order a Bloody Mary. A double. The two little bottles clink on my tray. I steady them and slowly unscrew their caps. The Indian woman asks for tea. No milk. No sugar. The stewardess places sachets of cashews next to our drinks. I rip mine open and nibble the nuts. The Indian woman leaves her sachet untouched. I wonder when she will open it. Then she smiles at me and slips the sachet into the red bag with the glinting mirrors.

'For my grandchild in Singapore,' she says and lets the bag drop to her thonged feet. 'I know it's the long way round,' she adds. She sips her tea and her bangles tinkle. I feel her eyes on my wedding ring and tuck my hand under the grey blanket spread over my knees. 'Do you have children?' she says.

I hesitate. The thick red drink pearls down my throat. I nod. 'Two. Two girls.' My hand comes to rest on the small drawn-out tray and I grip the clear plastic cup.

The woman pats my hand. Her skin is soft and I smile weakly. I sip my drink. A taste of dried out tomatoes grates on my tongue. I bite back my tears.

'You look sad,' she says.

I clear my throat. 'My mother's husband died. I've just been to the funeral.'

'Your father?' The woman rocks gently in her seat.

'My stepfather,' I say. 'My father died ten years ago.' I close my eyes.

'I'm sorry,' she says.

The warmth of the vodka numbs the flesh in my mouth. I'm sorry, too. My father was a good man. A good father. And he was good to my mother. Our threesome was perfect. Then, it was untouched by the complications of a brush-fire passion.

The stewardess brings our food. She reaches a tray over to the Indian woman and says: 'Vegetarian?' The Indian woman nods. I watch her peel back the foil and her hand slips into the folds of her sari to draw out a vial, which she opens. I can smell coriander and curry as she sprinkles spices on stewed tomatoes and chokos on a bed of steamed rice. I stare at the food and then I feel a tap on my arm.

The man next to me is holding my tray. I notice his hands and say 'Thank you'. 'Red wine,' I say to the stewardess. Then I peel back the steaming foil of Beef Wellington. I don't know why I chose it, what I expected. The portion lies small and soggy in the corner of the high-sided plate. My cutlery slips from the sachet onto my lap. I squirm in a balancing act.

I had eaten Beef Wellington with Rob two days before I left London for the funeral in Sydney. It was the last of a series of meals we'd had together. It had all begun so easily. A drink after work. Then lunch. One lunch led to another. We talked about work, our families. Lunch time without Rob soon became empty. And then people began to talk.

Rob had never kissed me, although I did feel his lips brush my hair as he hugged me the day I landed my first big contract. We'd celebrated in a fancy hotel. He'd ordered my first taste of Beef Wellington, deliciously rare in a crisp golden crust. Heavy French wine, a Bordeaux, I think.

I glance at my neighbour. He has the same hands; they're small for a man, or that's how it seems. But the palms are generous, the fingers sensitive. He also wears a school ring on the little finger of his right hand. No wedding band. Just like Rob.

I plan on calling Rob from London before I take a cab home to my husband and daughters. I just want to say I'm back. Want to hear his voice. Hope he'll suggest a drink the next week. Hope he has missed me. I stare out the window as the brightness leaks into black and remember the dream David told me about just before I left for Sydney.

'I was so angry,' he'd said. 'We'd had friends over. You served them red wine. All the glasses were perfect but the one you gave me had a hairline crack. As I drank, droplets seeped through onto the table. You re-filled my glass. The crack widened. Burgundy drenched the front of my shirt. The white linen one you bought for my birthday. I leaped up and you laughed. I stormed to the kitchen. But there, the tiles had been torn from the walls and the sink was ripped out. Not even water to rinse with.'

I remember how he had trembled and then he'd said 'What does it mean?' I'd just answered: 'I don't know.'

The Indian woman stirs in her seat and her elbow brushes mine. 'My son is a good man,' she says.

Her amber eyes are sad. 'Where I live,' she says, 'we see many facets of a jewel. The cut of a sapphire has more than one edge.' Her skin is brown and patina smooth; it gleams against the pewter streaks of her hair.

I sip my wine. Sip. Think of David. Think of my pregnancy and how it couldn't have been easy with me as useless as a waterlogged balloon. David had been the first at his company to ask for paternity leave. They didn't give it, of course. Not fifteen years ago. Not even for a father of twins. It was when the girls were six months that we switched roles. David had always been a good father. He'd done more than just proudly stroll the girls in the park. He'd even opted to stay home when I began my career and started flirting with the glass ceiling. Yes, David was a good man.

I glance at the man beside me. His face is closed in his paper. A wife and children at home, no doubt. Secure in his own safe world, which seems to hold him in a steel embrace high up above the clouds. I shift and stare out of the window as we flee from the sunset. I think of my mother, her two good men.

'So your mother loved twice?' the Indian woman says.

I fumble for words. 'The timing was not...perfect,' I say. Then the words tumble out. 'People were hurt. It had been a long hot summer. No rain. The brush was dry. All it took was one spark. Luckily, we didn't lose all we had.'

The Indian woman looks at me and smiles sadly. 'Fire cleanses,' she says, 'but it can also bring devastation...'

The fasten-seatbelt sign comes on and I close my eyes. I think of my daughters and how I must tell them about the brush and the danger of it drying out, of flames that can flare out of nowhere.

The plane touches down and I become one of the many passengers spilling into the arrival lounge. Soon I'm caught up in the wave towards immigration.

Standing in line, I catch the scent of coriander. I turn and see the Indian woman. She raises her hands, palm to palm, to her forehead. Our eyes meet once more and she smiles.

In the baggage claim area I see a phone booth. Rob's number ticks through my mind. I turn towards the carousel just as my luggage comes down the ramp. Then I take my bags and walk from the airport.

The road outside gleams wet in the sunlight and I see the Indian woman cross to the car park. A young man carries her suitcase. A young woman, visibly pregnant, holds the old woman's red cotton bag. From a long black line an orange cab breaks out. It approaches, and I hail it.

As the taxi speeds off I think of my family waiting for me at home, of my husband, my daughters. I want to tell them about their grandmother. I want to tell them about timing, how a new fire can burn once an old one has died. I also want to tell them about back burning and fires that are lit to quell bigger flames.

And my husband, I want to tell him that I have been thinking a lot about his dream and that I have concluded that that's all it was—just a dream. I'll tell him tonight after the girls have gone to bed and we have a late night dinner, as we used to have when I came home from a trip. My mind is racing. I shall make a meal of chokos and chicken slivers on steaming rice, sprinkle it with coriander. I shall prepare him a meal fit for a rajah. I shall find the indigo sari I brought back from one of my trips—David loved seeing me wear it. It must be tucked away in my cupboard. I shall put on the golden anklet he gave me, and the thin gold bangles. The pulse points of my wrists I shall anoint with musk and the bangles will tinkle as I caress him.

Matroshki

I saw Miles off to Moscow in June. Summer hovered through the muslin of clouds and the clematis mauved over our front door.

'Try and ring,' I said.

'Won't be easy,' he said.

When he came back a day earlier than expected the clematis was in full bloom and hanging deep over the doorway. I was on the floor in the living room, the room where we lived, where we had loved. I was on my back, doing breathing exercises, my legs slightly apart, my head to the door. The sound of my breath expiring deep from my belly blocked out his footsteps. I didn't hear him come in. I opened my eyes, let them rise from the stuff of his twill trousers to his knees, the rise beneath his belt, the slight rounding of belly above. Then his knees came closer as he squatted above my head and bent to kiss me.

'You have pollen on your hair,' I said drowsily.

'It's the clematis. It's grown so.'

'I'm glad you're home.'

It was of course his work that took him away. Good interpreters could call the shots, and Miles was a linguist: Russian, French.

'You have to live language,' he would say. 'It's not just words; it's all the senses.'

Miles took care of himself. Always smelled good and looked it—even the designer jeans for after hours. He knew about senses.

Was it his vanity that made him stroll the dark streets of Moscow with Natasha? I remembered the words in my *Oxford. Vanity: unsubstantial or futile nature.* Futile. He must have known it would be futile. You don't pick up a good-looking woman in Moscow just like that. Or at least you didn't then. She wanted his dollars; they'd buy more than her rubles at GUM. Miles had told me about the store and about the women who lay in wait for foreign men from the West. He'd said he knew what the women were after. Said he was one step ahead and always kept one hand on his wallet. What had he been thinking? Or was he just being vain?

Only later would I work things out about Natasha. Not that Miles told me. I think I even made up her name. But when he showed me how the doll worked, that's when I thought I understood.

'It's a nest, really,' he said. 'You take one off and there's another inside.'

'And another. And another.'

'Yes.'

'Did you try to ring?'

'Yes,' he said. 'You weren't home.'

Miles placed the doll on the floor and sat down. Then he opened it. There was another inside. He handed it to me.

I examined the doll. Red feathery brush strokes made patterns and pleats on its painted skirts. I screwed the top off and took out the next doll. Spangles and flowers were recognisable. Small, but the petals were there. And so it went as I opened each doll in turn until I had placed at his feet a row of progressively smaller dolls, each one less distinct in its painted clothes.

'What's it called?' I said. I meant they, but they were all within each other. The name had to be generic.

'Matroshka,' he said and took the biggest doll and turned it round in his hand. 'These days the dolls can be anything. Politicians. Pop stars.'

'But originally?'

'Russian for mother,' he said.

'But why so many? One inside the other?' I took the smallest one, the size of the nail on my little finger; it was moulded in a pear shape. I wondered if Natasha's breasts were pear-shaped. Miles had always likened mine to inverted pears. Even in the early days. When they had been firm.

I tried to keep in form, but not with aerobics. Maybe because I had a distaste for the bright lycra uniforms that went with the public show. Yoga was more my game. Breathing exercises. The long deep breaths helped me expel the tensions of the day, the remains of the doubts that went through my mind during Miles' frequent absences.

Once, back from a mission, he'd peeled garlic cloves and placed them into little jars and filled them with oil. 'This is how it's done in Moscow. They don't always get garlic. Grab it when they can.'

I used that oil for cooking one day. The house stunk for a week. Miles frowned and then he was off again.

When Miles stopped bringing home spices I began doing my breathing exercises more often.

Then came the day when he brought home the dolls. The Spice Girls. I laughed. 'Capitalist decadence.'

His forehead furrowed and his eyes lost their lustre.

I asked him about the garlic. 'Do they still keep it in oil?'

'No. They can get it whenever they want now,' he said. 'Maybe I'm getting old.'

I surveyed the grey curling behind his ears. 'We both are, Miles.'

'And the Russians are going towards a new scene,' he said.

'You take things too seriously. It's only fresh garlic. Spice Girl Matroshki.'

He sat down on the floor by my side and crossed his legs. 'Show me how you breathe,' he said.

I stretched out on the floor, legs slightly apart. My hands feathered my abdomen, fingers spread gently, middle fingers touching. I closed my eyes and breathed in deeply. My fingers parted. I exhaled slowly. The familiar sound resonated through my ribcage as my fingers drew together to touch once again. I kept my eyes closed, but could feel Miles watching me. I took another rhythmic breath. As I exhaled I felt a warmth by my ear.

'Teach me,' Miles whispered.

I opened my eyes and turned to face him. His foot touched the Matroshki and I heard a faint rattle as the dolls rolled away.

Heatwave

It's cool up here, Tim. I had to get away. Gareth said we'd only be gone a few hours. A spin in his Cessna, away from the heat. That's all it was, Tim. Promise. I can see the green hills below. Some already curving into beds of blue heather. It's so cool up here, Tim.

Every day of the month I'd been back in London had been close and heavy. I wasn't used to heat waves in Britain, specially after the cool Christmas July of the Blue Mountains. Do you remember that Saturday morning, Tim? When we were sitting out on the porch? Remember? Remember the parcel the postman brought? From Australia. Surface.

'It's from Jacky,' you said and you turned it over and handed it to me.

I stared at the stamps of fluttering pink cockatoos strung out along the top.

'Joanna,' you said. 'It's postmarked a week before she died.'

All I could do was finger the brown paper. And you placed a hand on my shoulder for a moment, as if to steady me. Then you sat down on the steps and waited.

You were always so understanding. You understood my need to dash back to Sydney for Jacky's funeral. She was my best friend. You understood. You always understood. All my needs, even though I knew they must have hurt you sometimes.

Remember how I ripped off the brown paper? It was a book. The size of a missal. But the cover was kitsch. Hearts. Flowers. Angels. There wasn't a note. 'It's Jacky's diary,' I said and then I began to rewrap the paper. Remember? You stared at my hands, but I couldn't stop smoothing, caressing the creases.

You said: 'I'll leave you two alone then.' Said you had things to do in the garden. That the heat would kill the roses. Remember?

I watched you leave and I thanked you. Begged that you be off with your roses. Your bloody roses, Tim!

As soon as you'd gone I tore back the paper. I took a deep breath. Opened the book. At the last page. It was empty. So were the twenty or so before it. Then an entry dated a week before Jacky's death. Two days before the date of the postmark.

3 July. I coughed blood this morning. I can't tell you, though. You'd worry. It would only hurt you. I know I can't spare you the big hurt at the end, but I've always tried to spare you the little ones along the way.

Tim, I couldn't read on then. Why had Jacky sent me her diary? Why hadn't she left it for Doug? She must have had a reason.

Tim, Jacky died the day before her twentieth wedding anniversary. She and Doug had what we thought was the perfect marriage, or nearly. Apart from not having kids. But then, we didn't have kids either. Oh, I know, it wasn't your fault. I was always too busy. Too scared. Scared of what? you said. Scared. Does there have to be a reason? OK, our marriage wasn't perfect. You tried, I know. So did I, in my way. Yes, I did try. But I was scared. I don't know why. Maybe of losing it. Hell! How I hated your roses.

Tim, Jacky and I grew up together. We told each other everything. Well almost. OK, I told Jacky everything. She didn't tell me much. But you guessed that, didn't you. It was like that with us. You never told me anything either.

Did I tell you I left Sydney the day after Jacky's marriage? I left for the old country in search of something new. Ironic, isn't it. I found you, Tim. Time and distance stole my intimacy with Jacky. But you know how it is, Tim, those childhood bonds. The secrets we shared. Mine. Jacky must have known it too, or she wouldn't have sent the diary, knowing that its contents were for my eyes only. That makes me laugh. Burning cars. James Bond.

OK, to be honest, it was always my secrets we shared. Jacky's, I'd try and draw out of her. She never wanted it that way; preferred to bide her time and then surprise me out of the blue with one of her "confessions". I didn't always listen, though. Did I?

When I first cheated on you, Tim, I had to tell you. As if confessing my slip—and that's all it was, I swear it—we'd had a little too much wine and you were away—it wasn't as if you'd been there and I'd made a conscious choice for...what's his name? Doesn't matter now, does it?

In a modern relationship we should be honest with each other, I said. And anyway, I couldn't turn it back, could I? You hardly reacted. Remember? And when I said I was sorry you opened your arms to me. Christ! Why didn't you beat me? I deserved it.

You were never one to speak much, Tim. You were a sponge, soaking up my peccadilloes, always forgiving. And I made sure that you always heard about them from me first. I didn't want you to become the cliché of the husband who was always last to know. We were a modern couple, weren't we? Perhaps not ideal like Jacky and Doug, but nobody's perfect.

Tim, I went back to the first page of the diary.

Dear Diary, [it said] (Dear Diary [had been crossed out.] I shan't write to you anymore. It's not like it was when we were seventeen and I really thought you were there. Maybe I have to find you again, but 'Dear Diary' is so silly. Specially now that Joanna's left. I really was only ever writing to her through you. Telling you the secrets I couldn't tell her. Joanna was such a chatterbox. She never listened to me. Her secrets were always the ones worth telling and then they weren't secrets anymore. But now she's gone and I don't need you anymore. I don't even know why I started this new book.

Tim, what is this need to confess? Maybe that's why they have priests. You can't hurt them. They're enough removed. So removed that you make up sins because you have to tell them lies because if you didn't they'd think you *were* telling lies. That's what they want to hear. What anyone wants to hear. Isn't it? I guess even way back as a child I didn't ever want to hurt the priest.

Tim, you always thought what I needed and wanted was a child. I know you did. You don't have to blame yourself. Is that why you started with the roses? What sort of a mother would I have made?

Tim, I didn't want a child. Not yours, not anyone's.

Tim, I should never have gone up with Gareth. It was silly. But I wanted you to notice. Flying a two-seater over the mountains. The thrill of it. You wouldn't understand.

Tim, it's been so hot. Jacky and Doug didn't have a perfect marriage. Doug played around. Jacky knew. Jacky did her own thing. She never told Doug. It's all in the diary, Tim.

Tim, I only went up with Gareth for a joyride. Nothing more. Not really. It's getting hot, Tim. We're losing height so quickly. I'm burning, Tim.

Tim, I love you.

The Black Hole

Sister Loreto had a hard mouth, just like my grandmother's. She'd tell us about Mary and Jesus and then take us to chapel before we had lunch. She always stood next to me in the pew and I was sure she could hear my tummy rumble. On Fridays it would rumble louder because we'd have to stay for Father Stephen to hear our confessions so that we could go to Mass on Sunday with a cleansed soul.

I liked Father Stephen even though he'd make me do the stations of the cross for my venial sins: telling lies, being selfish. I liked the music of the Hail Mary, could race through it, trying to break the speed record with my eyes on the second hand of the clock over the chapel door. I didn't think about the words.

So when Father Stephen gave me the stations and two Hail Marys at each, it wasn't really like penance, even though I was hungry. I was able to concentrate on the sculptures that lined the walls of the chapel, the sculptures with their bright robes and pink skins, their skins too pink for a Christ's agony. I didn't know what agony could be like then and I suspected Sister Loreto didn't know either. I never questioned Father Stephen.

I never questioned my grandmother either, but I didn't like her. She came to stay with us for a few months when I had my first communion. That day for me was almost like being a fairy, in my white frilly dress with the puffed sleeves. Mum had made it especially.

My grandmother always wore black, even on that day. But she did give me a pearly backed missal, and I think it was the only day I saw her smile. It wasn't a real smile: the corners of her mouth were straight and not turned down as they usually were when she'd thump her chest with her tight bony fists.

'Why does she do that?' I asked Mum.

'She's praying for our souls,' Mum said quietly.

Then one day my grandmother was gone. Mum said she'd died.

'What about our souls?' I asked.

'They'll be fine,' Mum said and smiled. Then she kissed my head.

With my grandmother gone I began to miss Mass. Mum had said my soul would be fine, hadn't she? So missing Mass never bothered me much and I even forgot to mention it to Father Stephen. It wasn't that I didn't like going to Mass on Sundays, just that I thought I no longer had anyone to take me. No one except old Mrs O'Leary, the last person in our town to ride to church in a horse-drawn carriage. So I asked Mum if I could go with her. And she said yes.

I'd run up the road to Mrs O'Leary's, brush down her gelding and wait eagerly for the old woman to back out the sulky. Mrs O'Leary would let me sit right up there in a tiny space next to her and I'd stare straight ahead at the horse's black tail swishing against his shiny brown rump. The clip clop of his hooves, the sulky's rumble—it would rock me until we arrived at the church.

'Get down, girl,' Mrs O'Leary said. 'Get rid of that chewing gum.'

I grinned, cleaved the gum to the roof of my mouth and slid from the sulky to go into church. The church was always full and many of my classmates were there with their parents. I'd sit at the back with Mrs O'Leary.

'Have you been to confession?' Mrs O'Leary asked.

I nodded.

'Then you shall go to communion,' she said and patted my hand. 'I promised Sister Loreto I'd see to it.'

I nodded again. I still had the gum on the roof of my mouth.

When I went up for the host and opened my eyes, I saw Father Stephen had spotted the gum. All of a sudden his mouth went hard, just like Sister Loreto's, just like my grandmother's. And then my eyes dropped to the black robes peeking from under his white chasuble.

The next Sunday, Mrs O' Leary was ill and didn't go to Mass so I didn't either. 'It's not a sin, child,' she said. 'It wasn't your doing.'

But that afternoon Father Stephen came to our house; he asked why I hadn't been to Mass in such a way that my mother got mad.

'We're Lutherans here,' I heard her say in a low firm voice as she closed the door.

I was peeking through the front window and saw how Father Stephen's mouth went straight and hard. Then he left.

It wasn't true, of course. Mum was Lutheran all right, but my father just didn't go to church. He said he was a pantheist. He'd told me how the bush was his church now.

'God is in nature,' he'd say.

'So why do I have to go to a school with nuns, wear a blue uniform, go to Mass?'

'It was your grandmother's wish,' Mum said. 'She wanted you baptised.'

'For my soul?' I asked.

Mum nodded.

It was after that Sunday, when Father Stephen had come to our house, that Sister Loreto started telling us stories. She told us about a family that had gone to Mass, taken the train and arrived safely. Another family had gone to the beach instead.

'...and the other family, the one that didn't go to Mass, they took the train to the beach. The train crashed down a black hole and they went to Hell.'

Sister Loreto paused and her eyes swept the room as if she were searching for twisted debris. Then she gave me a long hard look.

I felt my hands get damp on my desk.

'We shall now pray for their souls,' she said and placed her hands palm to palm, closed her eyes, and chanted: 'Hail Mary, full of...'

I raised my hands to interlock the fingers, as if by squeezing tight all the spaces between them I might make a tabernacle to keep out the devil. I closed my eyes, but the lids wouldn't stay shut and I saw how the faint damp splotches on my desk disappeared in the hot air.

I was lucky. Our family never took the train to the beach. Dad would clamp me between his knees on the front of the Vespa. Mum would sit pillion.

Years later I saw Sister Loreto at the station down from the school. She looked stiff and old in her long black robes. There was a younger nun with her in a shorter grey habit. They were welcoming the new girls who then filed up the hill in their royal blue uniforms, the way I used to do.

The road by the convent school went on down to the beach. Traffic had got busy and a zebra crossing had been painted in front of the school entrance. The next day's paper said a car had come too fast. Sister Loreto had been alone. She'd just hurried the last of her girls over the road when the car caught her full on.

I never travel by train, and when I drive to the beach I slow down at the crossings...even when no one's there.

The Colour of Haze

'You know you can ask us anything.' How often Hans had said those words to Anna. It was the sort of thing he was proud of saying. Proud of the risk of his promise and ready to stand up straight once that risk had been taken. Hans had always taken such risks, for his country and for himself. In our new life, our new land, that promise seemed easy to make to a child. Or had he seen that risk, too, and dared once again to take it?

Anna must have been six when she asked, 'Why is the sky blue?'

'Reflection from the sea,' Hans had said without looking up from his paper.

'You just cannot see the sea from here, Liebchen,' I had said.

Anna looked around the room and then went to the kitchen window. Hans looked at me and raised his eyebrows as she rushed past him to the front window.

'You cannot see it, can you?' I said. She shook her head and came to my arms. 'That doesn't mean it is not true,' I whispered and looked at Hans who nodded slowly.

When Anna was seven I remember her asking: 'Why do they call the Blue Mountains blue?'

I glanced at Hans and said it was the haze of the eucalyptus that made them look blue from the valley.

One Sunday we left home early and drove to Katoomba. We stood at the lookout behind the Three Sisters, those crags peaking out of the bush that ranged a tangy grey blue for miles and miles. And the crisp fresh smell made the blue so true that it didn't matter that the Three Sisters were red.

It was only when we took Anna to the Snowies that I realised the Blue Mountains were not really mountains. Mount Kosciusko, a blunt seven-thousand footer, was real, and was covered in snow—almost like the Austrian peaks I used to know. The eucalyptus smell must have been frozen in the red resin badges the stunted snow gums wore so proudly on their white bark.

Anna did not ask further and I thought she had forgotten about mountains, the sea—about blue. But one Saturday we were racing over Tumble-Down-Dick Hill to the beach on the road that dropped down and flew up, leaving my stomach and surely Anna's almost plastered to the roof of the car. And on the crescent she screamed: 'I can see the water! It's blue, like the sky.'

Yes, we did try to have all the answers, even if some of Anna's questions came too soon or we answered before she asked. I tried to prepare her for what lay ahead, knowing I had to be fleeter than nature—and time.

Like the time I tried to explain a picture I found in her zoology book, but the look on her face made me see the shouldered monster of ovaries she saw as her words cried in my head: 'I can't have that inside me!'

I think it was then I first felt her doubting the answers. But she still asked questions, at the table.

Our small family always talked at the table. 'It is important to talk,' Hans used to say. But, since his heart scare a month earlier when he had felt dizzy and had gone proudly to lie down he had taken to eating his food in a more measured way; he would chew methodically so that his answers became merely a shake of the head, a grunt or a nod. I began to notice that empty plates were a good way to move out of a discussion.

One evening at dinner Anna blurted: 'Who's Hitler? What's a Nazi?'

I remember a loud silence as Hans slowly pulled his knife and fork erect on either side of his half-finished plate. Then he swallowed his mouthful and said: 'Why do you ask that?'

'Mary Simmons called me a Nazi at school today. Because of the play. But, it seemed nasty.' Anna's eyes flicked from Hans to me.

I wiped my hands on my napkin and rose to lean over for Anna's empty plate. Hans aligned his knife and fork on his plate and stretched it out to me. Fatty scraps clustered one edge.

'Nazis were Germans,' he said and then paused. 'But not all Germans were Nazis.'

'But what's a Nazi?' Anna insisted.

Hans cleared his throat. I could see a telltale pulse at his temple. 'That was the war,' he said. 'It is a long story. It is late. School tomorrow.'

Hans had stopped driving after his heart scare and I had just come back from fetching him at the station. As usual he was tired after the peak-hour train ride home. The streetlights were just coming on as we came in and I called out to Anna. There was no reply. I went to her room and found her sobbing into her pillow.

'What is wrong?' I said, but she would not answer. So I just held her and prayed that whatever it was would go away. No one talked at the table that evening, but just before bed, Anna told me what had happened.

'At school today I asked Mary Simmons why she called me a Nazi. 'You're German,' she said. I said I wasn't. She asked how come I got the part of Gretel. If it was on account of my blonde hair. She said all the books have Gretel with blonde hair. And it's a German name.'

'What is so terrible about that?' I said and stroked her head.

'She said all Germans were Nazis.... That they burnt all the Jews. So I told her I was Australian and had a paper to prove it and what was a Jew anyway?.... Mary Simmons didn't know. She just said the Germans burnt them all up.... Said you and Dad did.' Anna lifted her head. 'What's a Jew, Mum?'

'Hush, go to sleep now. It is late,' I heard myself saying. 'We shall talk about it another time.'

Hans had gone to bed early and so I went to sit outside in the warm December night and thought of another summer. The war was over and I was making my way on foot from the station to my village in eastern Germany. I had bread in my knapsack, a bottle of water. Hans was coming to fetch me. To take me away.

I was still on the main road when a man came towards me. He was thin and ragged and as he came closer he held out his hands. 'Wasser,' he said.

I gave him the bottle I had in my knapsack and held out the bread. I watched nervously as he gulped and then tore at the half loaf.

'I am German,' he said between mouthfuls. 'I've come from the camp.'

'Camp? What do you mean?' I said.

'I am German,' he repeated and took my shoulders. 'Communist.'

His eyes were wild as I tried to step back. Then he began sobbing. 'You don't know what they have done.'

I hadn't thought of that time since coming to Australia. As I sat looking at the moon a half day into the tomorrow of my past, I wondered how I was to tell my daughter all the things she needed to be told. I wondered when would be the right time.

It was a Saturday and Hans was out. The scarlet camellias were in full bloom as Anna came rushing into the house, her blonde pigtails flying. She was clutching a postcard.

'It's from Austria, Mum!'

She held out the card.

'I have an uncle?' she asked softly.

Tall white mountain peaks. No trees. All he had written was:

A short goodbye. A big kiss to my niece.

I tried to keep my voice steady, but I felt so fragile. 'It is from Otto, your Papa's brother,' I said.

'Dad has a brother?'

I went to the sideboard. Bruised camellia petals had fallen from their wiry stems. I swept them into my hand and propped the postcard against the empty vase. 'Yes,' I said.

'Tell me about him,' Anna said.

'Later,' I said. I needed to think, I needed time. I could feel Anna's eyes on my back as I wiped my dry hands on my skirt and went outside. She followed me, watched me as I clipped three red camellias in the crisp sunlight. Although she did not say a word, I could feel the questions in her mind.

That evening at dinner I pushed the card across the table to Hans. 'Anna collected it,' I said.

Hans stiffened, then gazed at the card and said to Anna: 'Otto was my brother. He is dead.'

Anna swivelled from Hans to me. 'But he can't be! He sent the card.'

My husband's lower lip began to quiver. 'For me, Anna,' he said. 'He is dead.'

I placed my hand on his forearm and looked sadly at Anna. 'Otto ran away,' I said.

Hans tensed and his face went the deep shine of resin on the snow gums. 'Ran away? A deserter! A coward!' he shouted and banged his fist on the table.

Anna's eyes opened wide, wider than I had ever seen them.

'Otto thought Hitler was wrong,' I said quietly. 'Sometimes it takes courage to run away.'

There was a smell in the air like old mouldy memories.

'What did he know about right and wrong?' Hans cried. 'He laughed in the face of duty! Laughed at my medals! Laughed at me!'

'Maybe he knew about the Jews,' I said softly. I had almost forgotten Anna was there as she craned forward to hear.

'The Jews? What have the Jews got to do with it?' The pulse at his temple was twitching madly. 'We didn't know about the Jews! We were not Nazis!'

'No, we were not, Liebchen. Nor was he. He took a great risk and he paid the price.'

Hans' face reddened a shade deeper. 'The price? Have I not paid the price, too? Even today?' His breath pumped out as the words came in a sudden rush: 'Now their stigma they give to the heroes!'

'He helped one get away,' I said.

'He helped a criminal! Do you think there were no criminals among the Jews?' Hans stared at me, his mouth open wide; he was blocked on his chair. Then his head rolled back and he toppled to the floor. I remember thinking that if I had just held out my hand that night, everything would have been all right. But I did not.

Then Anna and I were both on the floor. I clutched her to me with one arm as my hand brushed his eyes closed. We sat there an age, and there were no tears. They only came later.

After the funeral I took Anna for a walk in the bush. The living quiet was soothing. The earth smelled rotting though, almost fermented.

'It is a rich soil,' I said.

'What was he like, Mum?' Anna said quietly.

I stopped and gazed at my daughter. Her blonde hair, the high cheekbones. Then I hugged her close, so close, and we walked home in silence.

Back in the house I went to the bottom drawer of the sideboard and pulled out a large grey envelope. The flap peeled away easily and I opened it and handed Anna an old pink-edged photo. There I was, a young girl in my twenties, my head between Hans' dark complexion and the fair one of his brother.

'That's Otto?' Anna said, and I nodded.

As she handed me back the black and white photo my eyes started to glaze beneath the tears. 'You have much from your father,' I said.

The Past Present

In 1969, fires of anti-protest burned in Franz Muller's eyes.
'Look at them! These young people! They defy their elders, defy their country!'

'Is that a bad thing, Franz?' his wife, Klara, said. 'They do not want war.' She smoothed a strand of greying hair from her face.

'I would fight for this country. I would go to Viet Nam.'

'Was not one war enough?'

'But this land has given me so much.'

'Stop that now. You are over fifty. Stop talking about wars.'

He no longer felt young, but he did not feel old. Driven by some mad force he had worked to rebuild his life.

Franz Muller retired in 1981. From one day to the next he felt old.

'Why do you not teach? Take in some pupils? Teach them German?' Klara said.

'German? We came here to forget, Klara. We are Australian now.' Franz Muller had always tried to keep buried his mother tongue, stifling it in his efforts to adapt. But the longing to repay a debt to the country that had taken him in was stronger now. It had become a challenge to replace those of the past he had been unable to meet.

Perhaps Klara was right, he thought. Perhaps the time had come to dig out his German.

Franz bought German grammar books, prepared lessons with the discipline of drills. The local primary school sent him its pupils. They came in ones, in twos. The years went by and Franz's days were filled.

'It is hard,' he said to Klara one evening, 'but they want to learn. It will be easier for them later.'

One day, just before the long summer holidays in December 1991, the telephone rang.

'I've heard you teach German,' the man's voice said. 'I'd like to have lessons.'

'I keep to the school term schedules,' Franz replied. 'You would only have two lessons before the holidays. It would be better next year.'

'If it's all right, I'd like to start next week,' the man said.

As soon as Franz had replaced the receiver he set about preparing the first lesson for his new student. 'My first adult.' A low whistle escaped his lips.

Franz would never forget that first lesson. He was surprised at how easily his new student grasped German grammar. Franz's excitement at how quickly the man turned phrases into questions eclipsed the meaning of the man's words. Here was a student who understood the construction of the language. Franz suddenly felt he knew what fulfilment was.

'He will not be back,' Klara said after Franz bade the man goodnight. 'He was not here to learn German.'

'Of course, he wants to learn German. I am lucky to have such a gifted student.' Franz packed away his books. 'It is late and I am tired. A good tired,' he said, patting his wife's shoulder.

The student did not come back for his second lesson. Franz waited for the phone to ring as Klara prepared an evening meal of sauerkraut spiced with carraway seed. Traditionally, a winter dish, its sharp and sour smell piqued the appetite. In summer Klara served it as a salad. Franz heard the click click of the knife as she chopped the seeds. He sat back in his easy chair and took the evening paper from the cherry wood side table.

The headlines screamed: 'Nazi war criminals could be your neighbours!'

Franz sat upright. 'Klara!'

Klara rushed to his side, wiping her hands on her apron. He pointed to the page. A small insert on the reporter held the face of Franz's student.

'He came to my home to...spy! He thought I was a...'

'He thought he had a story and he saw he did not, Franz,' Klara said.

'He asked about medals. I explained that the Iron Cross was for bravery.'

'He did not come back, Franz.'

The Iron Cross, what good was it now? Franz thought. He remembered how he had cast the medal into the POW latrine in Dachau the day the Americans had brought him in, the day fresh wounds had ripped to his heart, making those of his heroism pale. The Americans, too, had been wrong.

The summer holidays were long, long enough for Franz to prepare himself for the new school year. He soon found his teaching rhythm again, but he no longer accepted adult students.

One evening, Anya Wizniewski, the mother of two of his pupils, came to collect their corrected homework. As she left, she kissed the old man on the cheek. 'Thank you for what you are doing for the children,' she said.

Franz drew back. He did not know her well. He was not used to kisses in Australia.

Anya smiled a quiet knowing smile. Her grey eyes caught the flutter of emotion beneath his clean-shaven cheeks.

'I do what I can,' he said. 'They will know enough by Christmas to be able to talk to their grandparents.'

Anya nodded as Franz showed her to the front door of the white suburban bungalow. She was like him, a "new" Australian, though thirty years separated their naturalisation certificates.

Her parents had gone to live in Hamburg after the war. She had gone even further afield. He watched her retreat down the lamp-lit street. In the daytime Franz's posture carried pride that made him seem taller, straighter than his 5-foot 7 frame. Now his head was bowed with the fatigue of the years.

'She has kissed me on the cheek,' he said to his wife. 'She has kissed me, thanked me.'

'She is grateful, Liebchen,' Klara said.

'But I bombed them. We flew over Warsaw. I killed her people, maybe her family.'

'It was long ago. You had no choice.'

Franz sank into his easy chair.

'What would have happened had you disobeyed? You did not know them. It was long ago...' Klara's voice trailed into the evening damp.

Franz cradled his head in his right hand. It was a strong hand—short trim fingers with square nails, broad, deep palm—it should have been able to hold his head. It had held the throttle, the gun controls, the head of a comrade to stop him from drowning in the icy Dneiper River. Now it trembled under the weight of the grey, balding head, heavy with sorrow.

Suddenly, he sat up, his eyes strong with anger. "Unter-menschen" they told us. We believed them.' He slumped down. 'They lied to us. They sent us out.' The words tremoured from beneath his white clipped mustache.

'It was a long time ago. You were young. What could you do?'

'They lied to us. The young...they trust. They spoiled a whole generation.' His hands gripped the armrests of his easy chair.

'Hush, Liebchen. She kissed you. She was grateful for the children.'

Two days later, Anya's children came for their lesson. The blonde teenage girl and her dark-haired younger brother sat opposite Franz at the table. The books, the tape recorder, not even his hearing aid distracted them as his words reached out to their minds.

'It is still too early for you to understand in German. But I shall give you a line from a poem I have taken a lifetime to understand.' The room was still as Franz spoke: 'Blindly following my goal, I see not the path I tread.' His eyes held theirs. 'Think about it,' he said. 'We shall talk next time.'

The children gone, Franz sat back in his chair. His whole body sighed. As his lids began to close, he felt the kiss of Klara's hand upon his cheek.

Viennese Blood

It was the happiest time of my life. The saddest time, too. I was seventeen. I had arrived from England to work for eight months in a grand Viennese hotel. I was excited. I would at last see the world. Get away from Turnham Green. Go farther than London.

It was early May when the train puffed into the grey hangar of the Westbahnhof. The other passengers bustled by me as I lugged my knapsack down the high steps of the train and stood lost on the platform. Suddenly, a large hand clamped on my shoulder. I almost jumped, turned and saw a tall stout man with red shiny cheeks.

'Kennes Brrowning?'

I nodded. 'Kenneth,' I said.

'I am Herr Klain,' the man said. 'Velcome to Wienna.' He picked up my knapsack in an easy swing. The knapsack dangled and his arm directed me outside. His other hand held my shoulder.

The spring sun almost blinded me as Herr Klain hurried to the black hooded taxis gleaming in a line. Then he tucked me and my knapsack into the back seat of the first car and took his place beside the driver. 'Elisabethstrasse. Gösserhof,' he said.

Herr Klain's head scraped the car's ceiling. I could hardly see between him and the driver, so I looked out of my window at the road rushing past.

'Do you speak some German?' Herr Klain asked and turned his balding head towards me.

I shook my head.

'Ah,' he said. 'That will be good practice for my Harald then.'

'Harald?'

'My son. He has your age,' he replied, settling back in his seat. He looked straight ahead until we drew up in front of a small hotel. We alighted from the taxi and he waited an instant. A man in shirtsleeves and a black bow tie, a long dark green apron over his black trousers, pulled at the shining brass handle of the heavy glass door.

'Grüss Gott, Herr Klain,' the man said.

Herr Klain nodded and ushered me in past the oak-beamed foyer to stairs curving upwards.

'Our apartments are upstairs,' he said. 'You shall have your own room. You shall share Harald's bathroom,' he added.

Lugging my rucksack, I followed in Herr Klain's long shadow.

At the top of the stairs a young fair-haired man lounged against the banister. He greeted us with a half smile. 'Grüss Gott, Papa.'

'Harald! This is Kennes,' Herr Klain said and caught his breath.

I nodded.

'Come, boy,' Herr Klain said to Harald. 'Prove your English. You must learn something in that expensive school I send you.'

'Welcome to...the Gösserhof,' Harald said as we reached the landing. He held out his hand.

I almost lost my balance as my rucksack slid to the floor. Disengaged, I grasped Harald's hand. 'Good to meet you,' I said.

Harald smiled that half smile again.

'Show Kennes to his room,' Herr Klain said. 'Get acquainted.'

The room was long and narrow. The width of a cupboard and a bed. The door opened outward. There was one window on the opposite side. Looking out on the cobbled street, I dropped my rucksack under the sill. Harald leant in the doorway.

'One needs not much more in this house,' Harald said. 'It is enough to be able to come back.'

I thought it was a strange thing to say, but I nodded.

'The bathroom is next door. I have made place.'

'Thanks,' I said. Then I smiled. Harald smiled back, but still stood in the doorway. And he stood as I unpacked my two shirts, my three singlets, my underpants. He watched me unfold them and flatten them out in the cupboard. I didn't know what to say so I didn't say anything, hoping that he'd leave me a moment to adapt. When I had nothing more to put away, I faced him. 'And now?' I said.

'Now I show you my town,' Harald said. 'Come.'

Harald took the stairs two by two and I ran after him. 'What's the hurry?' I said.

'You must make the hay while the sun is still shining,' Harald winked, then laughed.

We raced out the door, past the man in the green apron. I had a strange and wild feeling of freedom.

Suddenly Harald stopped. 'Take a deep breath,' he said.

We both stood with our hands on our hips and filled our lungs. Then we both buckled over with laughter, but I didn't know why.

'Come,' Harald said and raced ahead.

A group of four or five boys in dark blue shorts and shirts with kerchiefs around their necks, the ends held together in a leather toggle, swaggered towards us. They must have been about ten or twelve years old.

'Your cub scouts?' I said.

Harald raised his eyebrows.

'You know. Camping. Hiking. Hiking in the Vienna Woods?'

Harald nodded. 'Yes. Cub scouts,' he said. 'Of a kind.'

As the boys drew abreast Harald quickened his gait. I was almost out of breath when we stopped at a fountain in the middle of a crossing. Cathedral spires threw long shadows down upon us. I shivered. Harald splashed his hands in the water and then splashed his face.

'It's cold,' I said.

'But good.' Then he stared at me. 'Are you a Jew?'

I splashed my hands and wet my face as he had done. 'Why?'

'You have a big nose.'

'So do you.'

We both laughed out loud.

'Come on,' he said and slapped me on the back. 'Race you back to the hotel.'

He was off with me behind him, trying to keep up. At a block away from the Gösserhof, Harald stopped. 'Walk now. We must be serious.'

My friendship with Harald grew with each week we spent together. On Mondays, when I had my day off, he would dash in from school to show me new places. One day we sneaked into Saint Stephen's cathedral and hid in an empty confessional booth off the main altar.

'Tell me, my son,' Harald said. 'Have you sinned?'

I giggled.

'Sshhh,' he said.

'How can I tell you if you say 'Sshhh'?

'No,' I said and stifled my mouth.

'Have you, … my son?' I tried not to laugh.

'Not yet,' Harald said. 'Not really.' His voice was earnest. Then he nudged me. 'Let's go.'

Daytime in the hotel was spent learning as the head waiter surveyed me. The other waiters watched silently.

'Take a carp,' the headwaiter said.

'How?' I said.

'Just put your hand in the tank and...take a carp. Catch it.'

I rolled up my sleeves and grabbed for the slithery form. I managed to catch it. Pulled it out. The fish thrashed, slipped from my hands and landed on the sawdust strewn floor. The waiters roared.

'Pick it up,' the headwaiter said drily. 'Rinse it and give it to the chef.'

Behind my back I heard snickering.

The hotel waiters had set up a soccer team. I burned to join in.

'Why don't you play?' I asked Harald.

'They're rough. You should keep away.'

'But it's a game,' I said.

Harald shrugged.

When I asked Herr Klain if I could play on the staff team his face grew sad. 'I do not think you should,' he said. 'They are rough.'

I wanted to play badly. 'Let's go once, Harald. Just once,' I said.

The next Monday afternoon we changed into shorts and jerseys and went down to the field a few blocks from the Danube Canal. Six of the seven waiters were already there. Three against three.

'*Können wir mitspielen?*' Harald called out.

They stopped and looked at us, one of them pointing to both sides. Harald went to one, I went to the other. Then the game started. The ball came towards me and I braked it with my toe. I started dribbling towards the goal. I was in control. Suddenly I felt a thwack in my side. A word spat by my ears as I crashed to the ground. '*Sau Jude!*'

Harald was by my side and pulled me to my feet.

'What did he mean?' I said.

'Let us go,' Harald said and walked me away. Behind us, I heard snickering again.

'I said it was better you did not play,' Herr Klain said. 'You are a Jew.'

I stared at Harald's father. Harald sat on the stairs, his elbows on his knees and his head hanging down.

'Kennes,' Herr Klain said, 'it is sad, but some of our waiters, they are good boys, yes, but...they do not like Jews.'

'But how do they know?' I said. 'I look just like you. Like Harald.' I tried to find some relief. I looked over at Harald. 'I have a nose just like his.'

Herr Klain put his arm around me and reached out an arm to his son. 'It is unfortunate,' he said.

The next Sunday and all Sundays thereafter Herr Klain insisted I accompany the family to mass at Saint Stephen's. I soon forgot the soccer incident. Harald and I would exchange grins as we knelt and glanced over at the confessional boxes.

One day, Herr Klain took me with him to one of the neighbouring villages in Burgenland to place his wine orders. Glasses of golden wine were passed around in the damp cellars.

'Sip,' he said.

I saw him drink, but didn't see him spit the wine out. I took bigger mouthfuls. I swallowed.

'The boy doesn't know how,' the wine-seller said.

'You're supposed to spit it out, Kennes.' Herr Klain spat in a bowl. 'Like this.'

I nodded.

'He will learn,' Herr Klain said to the wine-seller.

'That type never learn,' the man said. 'Just like those types in the village we're stuck with.'

Two other men tasting wine in the cellar mumbled agree-ment. The words came to me in a haze. I wasn't like that. I noticed the men didn't spit out their mouthfuls. I swallowed mine.

As we came up to the fresh air, my head started to spin, and my legs wobbled.

Herr Klain laughed as I tried to walk a straight line. 'It is to taste wine,' he said. 'You're supposed to spit it out. Not get drunk.' And he clapped me on the shoulder. 'You will learn, Kennes.'

I was euphoric again. I wished Harald were there.

On our last trip, though I didn't know it, we saw a family at the entrance to the village. A woman in long dark skirts and a bright head scarf stood behind a makeshift stand and plaited the dried leaves of corn cobs. A man in a slouch hat squatted on his haunches, smoking. A child sat on the ground, drawing in the dust.

As we passed in Herr Klain's old Ford, I turned my head, kept watching the family. The two men from the wine cellar appeared out of nowhere and sauntered towards the threesome. They kicked down the stand. Herr Klain kept driving, slowly. I watched through the rear window as the child buried its head in the woman's skirts, as the man stood and his arms encircled his wife. The two men laughed, it seemed, and walked off. All the while Herr Klain had been silent, then he stopped the car in the middle of nowhere.

'Kennes,' he said. 'I do not think you should stay.'

'But I still have three months to go,' I said. 'I like it so much here. You. Harald. I love Vienna.'

Herr Klain sighed. 'It is best you go back to England.' His voice was cold. Final.

Harald came with his father to see me off at the station. He bear hugged me. 'I shall write,' he said.

Herr Klain swung my rucksack in the overhead strapping and dropped back to the platform where Harald and I stood. Then he hugged me. 'Leb wohl, Kennes,' he said and his hand patted my face.

Tears prickled my eyes as I stood at the window waving at the large figure of Herr Klain and the slender Harald by his side.

I must have fallen asleep just after Linz. I awoke to screams as the train pulled into Salzburg. Two uniformed men in khaki, a red band flashing on their left arms were shoving three or four of the other passengers before them. It was a family I had seen board the train in Vienna. I had wondered if they were from one of the Burgenland villages near the Hungarian border where Herr Klain and I had tasted the wine. They were dressed in a similar way, almost like gypsies, but the woman was without the bright colours and the clinking gold baubles. Why would gypsies travel by train anyway, and where were they going? I had fallen asleep thinking they couldn't have been gypsies.

I looked out of my window. One of the uniformed men was barking something at the huddling group of four. The other turned to the train driver and raised his right arm straight in a stiff salute.

I stared out past the platform as the train pulled off to the border. 'Farewell, Harald,' I said as tears rolled down my cheeks.

The Tschusch

M onday, 10th June, 1991. 11:00. Klagenfurt, Austria.
The Gasthaus was full as the swarthy man in a yellow slicker
with KRONEN ZEITUNG plastered on the back and the front
pushed through the glass door, his arms piled with papers.

'Want paper?' he said as he shuffled between the tables.

Gerald Bauer looked up from his beer, grabbed a daily from the
man's arm and shoved some coins to the edge of the table.

'Danke,' the man said.

Gerald ignored him and shook out the paper. Then, tilting his
head in the direction of the newspaper vendor now just out of earshot,
he said to his workmate, Josef Posbicil: 'That one's been around for
months and still can't speak German properly. Want paper!' Gerald
snorted.

'Give him time,' Josef said. 'Who talks to him anyway?'

'They don't want to talk. They just want to cash in,' Gerald said and
leafed through the pages. Then he stopped. 'There you go! Some Yugos
nearly burnt a house down. Tried to grill a goat in the cellar. It's all
here in the paper.' He flashed the open page at Josef. 'Think they're on
the hills above Split, get homesick, then squat by the dozen in unused
cellars.'

'And who rents them camp beds stacked like sardine tins?' Josef said.

'Yeah. Well that's smart. Getting some of the money back is how I
see it.' He swilled from his beer. 'They're sucking us dry. Come here to
study, they say. Who bloody well has to pay?' He placed his glass on the
table with a thud. 'The taxpayer! That's us! Gotta get some of it back.'
Gerald pointed his finger at his empty glass and mouthed 'Another'
at the waitress behind the bar counter. 'Anyway, they don't notice the
difference,' Gerald said and turned the page of the paper.

When the waitress brought Gerald's beer, she looked at Josef and
raised her eyebrows to see if his beer wanted topping up. Josef shook
his head.

'And look here,' Gerald said, turning the page. 'A bit of all right.

Girl of the week. Dunja. Bet Dunja doesn't dare show off her tits like that back home.' He laughed.

Josef drank the rest of his beer and wiped his mouth with the back of his hand. 'Better get back,' he said.

Gerald emptied his fresh glass in one go. 'Yeah,' he said. 'Or they'll bring in the Tschusch to do our work. They'll work for nothing just to get in.'

The two men stepped through the heavy glass door onto the street and crossed over to the construction site of the hospital extension.

'So why do you want to go down to Dubrovnik?' Josef said.

Gerald rolled up the paper and waved it at him like a baton. 'Cheap flights, mate.'

'You're crazy to go now,' Josef said. 'The place is splitting up.'

'The Yugos bounce back. Did after Tito.'

'But, they say there's going to be civil war.'

'Nah. They're OK where they are. And they'll treat me like a king.'

'Yeah?'

'Yeah! You should see what they lay on. You should see the brochures. I could never afford Dubrovnik before, but now, the pearl of the Dalmatian coast. Sun, wine. The best food brought from Belgrade... and the women.'

WEDNESDAY, 12TH JUNE, 1991. 16:30. KLAGENFURT, AUSTRIA.

Gerald picked up his plane tickets and his booking for the Dubrovnik Plaza just opposite the casino. On the way home from the travel agency, his eyes slipped over the larger than life posters advertising scant underwear.

'KRONE!' a yellow-coated man yelled, bunching newspapers in his hand.

'Go to Hell,' Gerald said. 'You can't even read.' Bloody Tschusch, he thought as he turned the corner to his one-room flat. They flowed in with their old American cars left over from the last war, patched up and packed with runny-nosed kids, the roof rack piled past all laws of safety. They should stay home.

A new poster greeted him on the siding by the house where his flat was. He stopped. **AUSTRIA FOR AUSTRIANS**. The light blue background of the Freedom Party's flag set off the young fresh face of its leader, Jörg Haider. Gerald gave the poster a quick glance then hurried to unlock the massive front door of his apartment house. But the gaze of the face seemed to bore into his back.

How does the joke go? Scratch the blue and you find the brown? Yeah, well they're wrong there, too. But Haider's got a point. Specially these days. Forget it, he thought. I'm off in a week for the good life. He smiled to himself. The Schilling was still strong and would be stronger now that everyone was shitting in their pants. Didn't call it the alpine dollar for nothing.

THURSDAY,13TH JUNE, 1991. 03:00. KLAGENFURT, AUSTRIA.

Screams woke Gerald Bauer. He leapt to the window of his fourth floor flat and looked down on the dimly lit street. Three figures were attacking a fourth. In the night, they all looked the same. Foreign cries reached his ears. Gerald turned and went to the toilet he shared with the next-door flat. Out on the landing he met his neighbour. 'Bloody noise. The Tschusch again...'

The man nodded.

Back in his kitchenette entrance he plucked two balls of wax from a small bowl, stuffed them in his ears and went back to bed. He needed to sleep; let them wipe each other out.

THURSDAY, 13TH JUNE, 1991. 11:00. KLAGENFURT, AUSTRIA.

'Going to vote?' Josef said.

'Might go for the FP this time.'

'But we always vote red.'

'Well,' Gerald said. 'Haider wants to do something about the foreigners...'

'You know what they say about Haider. Those meetings in the glen. Like Hitler used to.'

'Those times are over,' Gerald said. 'I mightn't vote at all. See how I feel. What's one more or less?'

'Workers vote red,' Josef said.

'Yeah? Well, I'm off to Dubrovnik. Gonna play roulette. Gonna win. Gonna have fun.'

'You'll lose. It's always the casino that wins. I saw that in Velden,' Josef said. 'Can't compete with the big guys.'

'I've got a system,' Gerald said. 'Red or black, then keep doubling up. Sort of like safety on the fence. Later cheval on four numbers. See?'

'Like the vote?'

'Aw, shut up.'

SUNDAY, 16TH JUNE, 1991. 10:30. KLAGENFURT, AUSTRIA.

On Sunday, the urns were already in the local school hall. Posters plastered the entrance: red for the Socialists, black for the conservative People's party, and blue for the Freedom Party of Austria. Gerald had intended to saunter by on his way for his late morning beer in the Gasthaus round the corner. Familiar eyes bored at him from one of the posters. He stopped. Then he turned in.

Three urns were placed on card tables in front of drafted citizens. He took one of the sheets and marked a cross against FP. Then he folded the sheet and dropped it into the centre urn, showed his ID and watched as his name was struck from the list.

I deserve a beer now, he thought and smiled smugly.

Josef was waiting for him at their table in the corner of the Gasthaus.

'Done my duty,' Gerald said.

Josef just nodded.

MONDAY, 17TH JUNE, 1991. 11:45. DUBROVNIK, YUGOSLAVIA.

When Gerald Bauer landed at Dubrovnik airport the sun was shining. He adjusted his Porsche sunglasses and waved to a black Ford.

'German?' the driver asked.

'Austrian,' Gerald said.

'Son is in Austria,' the driver said.

Gerald nodded. Another one. They all had some family there.

'Good,' the man said. 'Good in Austria. Soon war here. Why you come?'

'A man's got to have a holiday,' Gerald said, hoping the man would stop talking. He hated the way the Tschusch broke up the language. Hey, they did more than that. They raped his mother tongue.

At the hotel, Gerald paid the driver and gave him a generous tip. He smirked as the man nodded his head four, five times. Subservient bastard.

The girl at the reception had long jet hair. She welcomed Gerald. As she turned to get his key, Gerald took her in from head to foot, lingering on her small waist and full hips. But their women were something else, he thought. While they were still young.

As she gave him his key he let his fingers brush hers, then he gave her a long look. The girl smiled back warmly. Wouldn't mind getting my hands on that, Gerald thought again as he went to the lift.

He was in a holiday mood and raring to go. Stroll around the hotel, maybe go down to the cafés by the sea. Check out the casino.

Although it was still daytime, the casino was already open. Gerald looked round the room with the roulette tables. Three of them were closed, but croupiers in their white shirts and bow ties stood at the ready behind another four. Two or three patrons, dark-haired and in tie-less dark suits, stood at each table, muttering in a vaguely familiar language.

Must be locals, Gerald thought. A wonder they let them in. And the money? Must be what they bring back from Austria. And we pay them!

Taxpayers' money and all they do is gamble. They'd never let these guys in at Velden. He watched as the men piled their chips on the numbered squares. Gerald looked around him. No other tourists.

They're probably all down the beach, being served by the Yugos. Sunning and watching the girls walk by topless. Our girls, that is. Theirs are all covered up. Except for Dunja back on page 3 of the *Kronen Zeitung*. His mind slipped to the girl at the reception.

He was feeling lucky. So he changed a wad of Dinar notes and went over to one of the tables. Two of the men moved aside as he kissed his fingers and placed a handful of chips on red. All Gerald heard next was the croupier's French of '*rien ne va plus*' and then his whole world exploded.

When Gerald came to he was lying in a hospital bed. He couldn't move, but his legs felt like they were being ripped slowly from his hip joints. He screamed. '*Scheisse!!*' All around him bloody wounded figures were moaning. He heard the sounds, but couldn't make out the words. A cocktail of panic and pain rose up inside him. He was alone in a roomful of Tschusch! No one would understand him! They probably didn't even know how to help him! What had happened? If only the pain.... He moaned and tears trickled from his half-closed eyes.

From the next bed he heard a muffled voice and turned to look at a bandaged head.

'You lucky. Got leg,' the man said.

Gerald felt pain. 'What do you mean?'

'Hit,' the man said. 'Wanted cut leg off.'

Gerald whipped his head from left to right. 'Where am I?'

'Dubrovnik.'

Dubrovnik. No doctors. The pain of Gerald's leg pounded in his heart. He closed his eyes. Just Tschusch.

Soft footsteps stopped at his bedside. 'German?' a calm voice said.

Gerald squinted up at a tall white-clad figure.

'You're lucky to be alive,' the man said. 'Dubrovnik has been bombed. We must evacuate.'

'You speak German?' Gerald whispered almost in relief. 'My leg...'

The man filled a syringe and swabbed Gerald's arm. Why didn't he answer, Gerald thought, his eyes searching the man's face, watching the man's hands.

The needle found his vein and Gerald closed his eyes once again. The last thing he felt was a warm fuzzy flow.

The last thing he heard was: 'Yes, I speak German. I studied in Austria.'

The Ferris Wheel

It was in Vienna I met him, in the Prater, that mad fairground bordering broad avenues where locals walked their dogs by day and whores offered their goods by night. I was on the giant Ferris wheel, the only ride on which I felt at ease, when he jumped into the cage as the wheels slowly turned.

I had been hoping to be alone, to slowly pull up to the top where the buckets sway and you can see the spires of Saint Stephen's, the Schönbrunn castle where Sissi tried to be Empress before she was stabbed in a foreign land.

He pulled at the door of the wire cage and stepped in.

'May I?' he said. I shrugged. I could hardly say no. I remember thinking he must have been a local to break through the barriers.

'I've been watching you,' he said. 'I've seen you often.'

It was a statement. What could I say?

Then he surveyed me. 'You're not from here, are you?'

I shook my head.

'Don't worry,' he said. 'I'm harmless.'

I nodded, averting my eyes, and the wheel churned upwards.

'Look at that view!' he said. 'All Vienna at your feet.'

I scanned the horizon and everything was still. But, down below, the Prater was alive, with its booths and rides, the sausages, the beer, the chips, the kebabs and the fairy floss, the ghost train, the big dipper roller coaster. And the dealers, though I didn't know it, then.

As he looked to the side, I glanced at his profile, his blonde hair just grazing the blue denim collar. Then he turned and I quickly looked out over the other side. The Danube below wasn't so blue.

He moved closer. I shifted. He moved back and said, 'Sorry.' I tried not to look at him.

There was something about him.

But I felt a kind of...I didn't know what.

Electricity? Pleasant, but scary. The four-minute ride felt stretched into hours.

At the top he thrust out his right hand. 'My name is Wolfgang.'

I took his hand. It was warm, firm. Then I drew back.

'What's your name?' Wolfgang said.

I'd never been asked so directly, so simply, not since I was a child. 'Gwen,' I said.

'Guewen.' He said it in a long way, as if he were tasting it. 'Unusual.'

No-one had ever called me unusual. Never to my face.

But he meant my name, didn't he?

No-one had ever called my name unusual.

The wheel inched on to its descent. I was feeling a buzz. Somehow, I just wanted to go round and round.

'Have you ever been on the looper, the roller coaster?' Wolfgang asked .

'The big dipper?' I shook my head.

Wolfgang opened the door of the cage and got out. When he held out his hand, I took it again. 'Will you have a beer with me?' he said.

I nodded slowly.

'Ha! I knew I could persuade you,' he said. 'Come this way.'

Wolfgang led me through the fairground, heading for one of the beer stalls. On the way, he stopped at the giant octopus. I shook my head. He stopped again at the ghost train, but I shook my head once more and said the screams made me glad to be on the outside. Wolfgang laughed and dragged me on. When we got to the beer stalls he bought two Gössers and while I drank sipping the strong dark beer from a clear plastic cup, he smiled and said: 'The mirror maze then?'

I gave in. We finished the beer and went across. When we got there, from outside I could see couples laughing and giggling at their distortions, feeling their way against the clear panes. Standing below, I could see the way out.

'I'm right behind you,' said Wolfgang. His hands rested on my hips. It was nice. Exciting. I stretched my hands out straight before me. My eyes, wide open, were blind to the turns, yet I still found a passage and we laughed at the reflection of two keg-like forms wearing our clothes. We were everywhere, nowhere. Another passage. A left turn. No right one. I bumped my nose and Wolfgang bent to stroke it. Then he kissed me. It wasn't really a kiss, more like a flutter of butterfly wings.

Then he said 'Let's try the big dipper.'

I'd always been terrified of roller coasters, even as a child. I'd never have got on by myself. But Wolfgang took my hand and squeezed it. I found myself squeezing back. Then his lips brushed my hair.

Still holding my hand, Wolfgang took the first row.

When I hesitated his grip became firmer. 'Come on,' he said, easing me in. Then he slipped an arm around my shoulders.

The roller coaster creaked upwards like an enormous centipede, each foot locking then unlocking on the chained teeth of the rails. It slowed as if for breath on the summit of the greatest loop. I couldn't have imagined what it would be like to go way, way up and reach such heights and teeter out of control in screams of glee and fear, yet held firmly in check by endless links of metal. The long metal beast tugged around and up and around again. I sucked in cold air.

The looper gripped with its myriad feet and paused at the top. Then my heart jolted to my throat as it hurtled into a fall, twisting, turning, bucking in every bend. Down.

Around. Up again. Around. Then down. And then trapped in its own mad momentum, in a desperate attempt to climb again, straining at the rails, it jolted one last time and petered out with tiny impotent clutches as it faded to a standstill. I let out the air.

My heart pounded somewhere in my throat and I clutched my stomach as the roller coaster eased to a standstill. I tumbled out, drunken.

'You'll get used to it,' Wolfgang said as he steadied me.

The next Saturday at the Prater I saw Wolfgang again. We rode the Ferris wheel, strolled around. Then we stopped in front of a shooting stall where the stallholder was barking: 'Six shots. Any prize...' When he saw us he gave me a strange grin then turned to Wolfgang. 'Hi Wolf,' he said and held out one of the rifles. I looked away and then down as a creamy something scurried into hiding in the cage at his feet.

'It's his pet,' Wolfgang said, taking the gun.

'A hamster or a guinea pig?' I asked.

'Same difference,' he said and cocked the rifle. Then he turned and winked. 'I think it's a hamster.' He took aim at the black and white bull's eye and the gun cracked. Once. Twice.

The hamster sat trembling in its nest of dark yellow straw, cut off from the door by a latticed cylinder.

Bang! Bang! Bang! Bang!

Wolfgang handed the rifle back to the stallholder and, as if welcoming me to his circle, held out his hand. 'Pick what you want,' he said.

Oversized shocking pink bears filled the backdrop, plastic watches and cheap costume brooches and bangles were crammed in the front showcase. A faint whirring sound drew my eyes to the hamster. It was going around and around in its tiny wheel.

Wolfgang drew close. 'The hamster?' he whispered.

I nodded.

'The hamster,' he said to the stallholder.

'Not a prize,' the man said and wiped the back of his hand under his nose

Wolfgang took out his wallet, opened it slightly. 'How much?' he said and pulled out a green 100 Schilling bill.

The stallholder smirked at me, then said to Wolfgang: 'One fifty, with the cage and the wheel.'

Wolfgang laughed, and held out the money. The man hoisted the cage over the counter and grabbed at the bills.

Wolfgang picked up the cage and swung it gently and, as we turned to leave, he murmured: 'Walk you both home?'

I nodded and let him take my hand. But I couldn't help feeling the stallholder's eyes on my back as we walked away.

My room looked over the fairground. Wolfgang helped me settle the hamster in a corner under the window and we watched as it sniffed at the air and burrowed into the damp straw. Then we made love.

Wolfgang didn't turn up the following Saturday. The one after, he sent flowers, blue cornflowers, with a note: 'Wait for me.' He came two weeks later. We spent the whole weekend in my room. The floor was our bed, our table, my heaven.

Then he was gone. But the letters almost made up for it. Nothing long. I never asked where he was the rest of the week, the weeks he didn't come. In one letter he added a photo of himself and a quote from Auden: "The desires of the heart are as crooked as corkscrews." I wondered if he were married. I never asked. I longed for him.

During his absences, I'd talk to the hamster. I'd stroke its soft pale fur, hold a fingertip to its twitching nostrils and then let it run round and round and round in its little wheel. Round and round.

'Don't you get tired of it?' I asked. It got off its tiny wheel and seemed to look at me for a moment. I thought it had heard me, understood something. Then it twitched its nose and burrowed back into the straw.

My relationship with Wolfgang had been going for about three months. It was a Saturday and though he'd not contacted me for over a week he swept me off my feet again with flowers, roses this time, and perfume.

'I want you to look very special tonight,' he said. 'There's someone I want you to meet.'

My heart danced and spun.

'Put on some high heels, something in silk,' he said.

I felt electric. I slipped on a white silk blouse and a black velvet skirt, sheer black stockings and my highest black heels.

'Perfect,' he said and kissed my head.

'Who are we meeting?' I said.

'Someone important.' He took my hand and lightly kissed it.

The ambassador directed his driver to a posh club in Baden about half an hour from Vienna. The three of us settled into a hidden alcove hung with burgundy velvet drapes.

'I have to leave now,' Wolfgang said. 'Trust me,' he added as he stroked my cheek with his forefinger. 'I'll be back soon.'

I nodded. What else could I do? The ambassador, a slight genteel man in his fifties smiled warmly and took my hand. He ordered champagne. We sipped. When he slipped his hand under my skirt and it ran up my thigh, I was numb. His small fingers grazed my neck and dipped into my blouse.

Where was Wolfgang? I thought. Why didn't he come? And then the room started to spin. Faster and faster. It was going too fast. I felt stuck to the walls. A sweet cloying smell moved in on me like the night fog. I tried to pull away.

Then the spin slowed and I felt myself falling.

As he had promised, Wolfgang returned. The ambassador brought us back to Vienna. 'Thank you,' he said, more to Wolfgang than to me.

In my room, Wolfgang took me in his arms. 'You'll get used to it,' he said. I trembled.

Then he held me and kissed me, so gently, so gently.

'Why?' The words grated from my throat.

'Because I love you,' he said. 'You're so fresh, so unusual.' Then he left .

I stared about me. Bile rose in my mouth as I rushed to the toilet then went to the basin and rinsed my face. I flopped down on my bed and saw the hamster. It was whirring in its little wheel.

Wolfgang had said he would call in a week. I had a number where he said I could call him, but I'd never used it. I slipped the scrap of paper from my wallet. The inky digits were blurred from where the creases of folding and unfolding had rubbed at the texture of the paper. Slowly I crumpled it until it was only a tiny ball and flicked it in the bin.

Left were the letters and his photo. I lit a match and touched it to the corners. The photo didn't want to take straight away, but as I watched the flame flickered then licked, swallowed, an ear, an eye until it raged through the head of blonde hair. The blue ink of the tightly looped writing gave less resistance than I thought it would. The letters weren't many. Black parchment ashes curled in the ashtray.

It was that time of the year when dusk sneaked in early and hovered about. I went to the window. The hamster had stopped spinning and sat tucked in the corner of its cage, nibbling from its dish. The roller coaster was still. There were no more riders. I watched as the ticket collector closed his booth and walked away. The Ferris wheel, too, stood motionless, gazing over Vienna. The streetlights went on.

When the phone rang, I clasped the receiver, held it an instant just out of its cradle. Then I hung up.

Grow Up

It's not that I ever wanted to be anything when I grew up. I just didn't want to grow up.

So when grownups didn't get an answer to the 'be' question straight away, they asked the 'do' question.

'I want to fly. Like Peter Pan.'

'You want to be like Peter Pan?'

'No. I want to fly like him.'

When I was told that Peter Pan never grew up, I said, 'I don't want to either.'

'But, Pamela, you have to grow up. Everyone grows up.'

'Why? What if I don't want to?'

'It's the way of nature, darling,' my mother said.

My mother was grown up. But I could talk to her in spite of that. In a way she was right. Nature started doing things without me being able to stop it.

'My, how Pamela has grown, Mrs. Thomson,' one of the neighbours said.

So? I was getting taller. I seemed to need new shoes before I wore out the old ones. I could handle growing up after all, I thought, if it meant new shoes all the time. It also meant breaking them in, getting blisters on blisters. Maybe my feet should stop growing for a while. When the blisters hurt, I'd say to my mother: 'Mum, I don't want to grow up.'

'That's just growing, darling,' she'd say. It seemed a lesser evil.

I kept growing and my breasts formed and I got my first period.

'Pamela is growing up,' I heard my mother say to someone on the phone.

So that was growing up. Well, I could do without it. I could do without things that bobbed when I ran, not being able to swim at that waterhole at a certain time of the month, pimples bursting out on my face at odd moments. I'd cry for nothing, before I knew why. Growing up was the pits.

When I poked out my tongue in class, the teacher said, 'Pamela, do grow up.'

When I sulked, I was told to grow up. Being grown up was something my friends wanted to be. They said they could wear high heels and stockings and go into town alone. Big deal. I'd rather fly.

So I climbed up on a rock and tried it. Luckily it was at the waterhole. I started thinking the grown ups could be right. That I had no choice. Or did I?

What was so great about being grown up? The adults I knew didn't seem so thrilled about it. They were awfully serious most of the time. The things that escaped them that made me laugh, they sucked in again.

I managed to make it to sixteen. I grew up on the outside, began flying on the inside. I think my mother understood. She'd smile and shake her head when she caught me miles away.

Then I fell in love. I thought I'd grown up inside. I'd sit around and dream all day. I'd love everyone, smile everywhere.

Mooning, they called it. 'Grow up,' they said.

I married my love. Now she'll grow up, they said. I felt expectation breathing about me. So I started playing the grown-up game—with one concession: I'd answer the phone 'Neverland here. Looking for the lost boys?'

It didn't last long. 'Grow up,' said my husband.

My daughter was born. Part of me grew up. A bigger part of me went to play with her.

'Who's Peter Pan, Mum?'

I told her the story.

'But, Mum. Everyone has to grow up. I can't wait till I'm nineteen.'

'Oh it's not a matter of age, my darling,' I said. 'It's in the mind.'

She gave me a quizzical look as I prayed she'd understand one day.

Maybe it was because I never grew up that my husband left me.

'You know, you are a bit strange, Mum,' my daughter said to me one day in her late teenage wisdom.

My pre-menopause friends said, 'Pamela, you ought to grow up, you know. You can't always say and do as you please.'

'But I'm not hurting anyone.'

I'm a grandmother now. Would you believe I've fallen in love? I ride rainbows with leprechauns, wear purple under-wear. Somehow nobody seems to bother anymore. It suits me like that. I blow bubbles and raspberries wherever I choose and my world is full of indigo and cyclamen. My grandchildren understand me.

Friends and Lovers

G reg and Sandra had been friends since way back, well, not back that far but back far enough. Just since the day they'd met as expats in a bar in Earl's Court, London's Kangaroo Valley. Neither had meant to hang out with other Australians, but when a can of Fosters and a Vegemite sandwich weren't strong enough to keep away the homesickness, where else was there to go? Neither admitted to loneliness. They just started talking. Found they liked the same films. The same food. Both wanted to find the Europe of their dreams.

'It's so great to be able to just talk,' Greg said one evening over dinner in Sandra's bedsitter.

'Yep,' Sandra said. 'It's nice. No ties.'

'I'd just broken up when I met you,' Greg said. 'One of the reasons I left Australia.'

'Didn't want to get caught on the rebound, eh?' Sandra said.

'How did you know?'

'Happened to me, too,' Sandra said. 'Want some dessert? I've got some trifle.'

'Love trifle,' Greg said and grinned.

Greg helped with the washing up and then left before midnight. 'Thanks, mate,' he said and gave Sandra a hug.

'See ya later,' Sandra said as she waved from the door.

Greg and Sandra grew close. Close, the way only children imagine having a brother or sister could be in the best of all possible worlds.

When Greg went to Sweden, Sandra headed for France. They kept in touch with regular phone calls. With postcards. They'd meet when Greg passed through Lyon, when Sandra could detour to Stockholm, always picking up naturally where they'd left off.

'How's your love life, Greg?' Sandra said on one of his side trips to Lyon.

'So, so,' he said.

'But what about those Swedish girls?' Sandra gave him a sly look.

'Guess it's like everywhere' Greg said. 'How about your Frenchmen, a change on the Aussies?' He winked.

'Hmmm. Sort of,' Sandra said.

'Anything serious? You can tell me.'

'Give it some time, Greg.'

'So it is serious. What's his name?'

'Alain,' Sandra said and reddened.

When Sandra married Alain in Lyon, Greg couldn't be her best man; nor could Sandra be Greg's matron of honour at his wedding to Britt in Stockholm six months later. But both attended the other's wedding as the other's best friend. Greg and Britt came twice to Lyon. Sandra and Alain went to Stockholm, one, two, three times. The third time was just after Greg's daughter was born.

'Why don't you come more often?' Greg said on the phone one day.

'Why don't you?' Sandra said.

'Well, it's hard with the family. Natasha seems to be growing before my eyes. And Britt, well you know Britt, how she doesn't like me to leave.'

'I don't really know Britt,' Sandra said. 'She hardly says a word to me.'

'She's shy. Worries her English is no good.'

'But she can when she has to.'

'Well, look at your Alain. Hardly a word either,' Greg said.

'Alain can't,' Sandra said.

When Alain walked out on Sandra and the divorce came through, Greg came to Lyon.

'I can stop over on the way to London,' he'd said on the phone. 'Just for the weekend—to toast your new freedom.'

Sandra laughed. 'Lucky I didn't have kids to tie me down,' she said.

When Greg's marriage broke up, Sandra flew to Stockholm and Greg wept in her arms.

'Guess we both married the clichés of our dreams,' Sandra said.

'It's not that,' Greg said. 'Just because I don't have faith in her as a woman, my woman, doesn't mean she's a bad mother.'

'Didn't mean to be smart,' Sandra said. 'And I'd forgotten your daughter. That makes it all different, doesn't it?'

'I don't want Natasha to suffer. I want to stay friends with my wife.'

'Your ex-wife.'

'With Britt.'

'Think you can?' Sandra said.

'It won't be easy, but if we're not selfish...Britt said she was ready to try, for Natasha's sake.'

'I really admire you,' Sandra said. 'Don't know if I could do that—what's over is over. But then there's Natasha...'

One Friday morning Greg phoned to say he was coming to Lyon for the weekend and would be arriving that evening. Sandra dashed out and bought fresh flowers and food from the market, and put her best sheets on the double bed. Then she put another set out for the couch.

'It's so good to see you, mate,' she said as he stood in her doorway. 'I've got quail and wine...'

Greg laughed. 'Hey. Slow down. Let me come in first.' Then he put down his overnight bag and hugged her. 'Good to see you, too, mate.'

Over dinner they spoke of their lives. 'Isn't it strange,' Sandra said, 'how you always can only be friends with one of a couple.'

'You mean you and Britt?'

Sandra nodded.

'Me and Alain?'

'Yes.'

'Let's enjoy this then,' Greg said. 'Show me your old town.'

Sandra slipped on her jacket and hand in hand they skipped down the stairs of the old apartment house in the middle of town. It was too early for tourists and the glow of the lit-up cathedral twinkled over the river. They strolled along the embankment then turned back to Sandra's apartment.

'It's nice here,' Greg said.

'When you're not playing tourist.'

In the doorway of Sandra's apartment house, she fumbled for the key. As she slid it into the lock, Greg kissed her.

Sandra slipped from her bed the next morning to make coffee. The small pile of sheets for the couch were on the floor. In the kitchenette, she hummed as she heated three croissants and poured milk coffee into two breakfast bowls. Then she smoothed her hair and carried the tray back to the bedroom.

'Coffee time,' she said.

Greg stretched. 'Espresso?'

'French coffee and croissants,' Sandra said with a smile.

'But I like espresso—in small cups, ones with handles,' Greg said, pouting. Then he grinned.

'Should've guessed,' Sandra said. 'You never got espresso too easy in Stockholm, did you.'

She placed the tray on the foot of the bed and came to kiss him.

At the airport on Sunday, they held each other. 'Come to Stockholm for Christmas?' he whispered against her hair.

'Britt will be there?'

'Yes, but with her new man. Family,' Greg laughed flatly.

Sandra kissed him. 'I'll be there.'

There's something magical about Christmas in Stockholm, Sandra thought as her plane came down in Arlanda. Lights glowed and twinkled against the snow.

'I've invited some friends,' Greg said at the airport. 'You know, ones with no home for Christmas.'

'Like me?' Sandra asked quietly.

'Like me,' Greg said and hugged her close.

All the windows of Greg's apartment house glowed warmly with Christmas candles. The scent of nutmeg and cinammon was in the air.

'It feels just like Christmas, how I imagined it,' Sandra said.

'Wait till you taste it,' Greg said. 'Turkey and ham, and *Glögg*.'

'*Glögg*?'

'Hot mulled wine. That will keep your Christmas spirits up for days.'

'No Vegemite?' Sandra said.

'Gotta be joking.'

As Sandra came into the flat, a five-year old girl edged close to her mother on the couch.

'Hi Britt,' Sandra said as the blonde woman rose.

'*Hej*, Sandra,' Britt said and held out her arms. The two women hugged. 'Come, Natasha. It's Sandra. A friend of your father's.'

Sandra dropped to her knees. 'Hallo.'

Natasha smiled shyly.

'This is Sven,' Britt said and waved a hand towards a blonde bearded man on the couch. He nodded.

Sandra said '*Hej*.'

'How can you bear it?' Sandra said to Greg in the kitchen after the meal, when they were alone. He washed as she dried.

'It's all very civilised, isn't it?' Greg said.

'But seeing him here with her?'

'It's her life. It's tougher on him, I suppose. I have Natasha.'

'But not all the time.'

'No. But it's better than nothing. I am her father.'

Sandra shook her head.

Their lovemaking that night had a certain edge.

'I don't know what it is. It feels like Christmas, but a Christmas for families.'

'You mean, not for lovers?'

'I don't know,' Sandra said.

The next day was spent with Sven, Britt and Natasha. Two couples, one child. But Sandra was the one who felt left out. When she left to go back to Lyon, she hugged Greg and said: 'Come see me soon?'

Greg nodded and kissed her. It reminded her of one of Alain's last kisses.

Sandra didn't hear from Greg for over a month. Then he phoned.

'Sandra, Britt and I are getting married again.'

Sandra held the receiver away from her ear.

'Sandra?'

'Yes.'

'Did you hear me?'

'Yes.... What about Sven?'

'Nothing serious,' he said. 'And it's best for Natasha. Aren't you happy for me?'

'Yes, Greg. I'm so happy for you.' Her voice rang dull.

'Divorce is so easy,' he said. 'Maybe we rushed things.'

'And you became friends,' Sandra said.

'But never friends the same way as with you,' Greg said. 'Britt and I were... well, we were friends for Natasha's sake...'

'But you were always just...lovers. Is that it?'

It took a while for Greg to answer. 'Yes,' he said.

'Thanks for letting me know, mate,' Sandra said. 'See ya later.'

'We'll be sending an invitation. To the wedding. You won't have to pay. That's our honeymoon. Having our friends.'

Sandra was silent.

'Have to go now. Love you, mate,' were the last words she heard.

Sandra spent ages looking for the right gift for Greg and Britt. She wanted something simple, something practical, something that would fade into the household. She bought two bowls, ones without handles, ones the French use for breakfast coffee. They could use them for dips or chopped onions, she thought. Two mustard ones, the stock colour in the supermarket.

She packed them securely.

Then she mailed them with a card to apologise, to say she wouldn't be coming.

Bobbin Head

They didn't call them corporate ladders back then, but I guess, in a way, Dad taught me to climb them.

I grew up in the suburbs of Sydney when they were still country and the bush came up to the back door. In our street we were eight kids. I was the only one who had to squat to pee. But that didn't matter because down the bush there were always enough eucalyptus trees and bottle brush bushes for cover.

We were tough. In the summer it got so hot that we'd never wear shirts or shoes. Our soles were like leather by the time we went back to school and it was hard forcing our feet into lace-ups.

I called myself "Bill" and when Mum bought me T-shirts and shorts, I made her swear they came from the boys' section of the store. She'd swear, and smile. And I'd keep my face straight.

Maybe I was one of them because of my billy cart. We'd scavenged old fruit crates. Dad had made the axle, but let me nail the slats of wood together. I missed a nail, slammed my thumb, but I bit back the tears, and when the pain died down I wore the bruise like a battle scar. Dad put ball bearings on my cart as wheels and said it would be the fastest in the street.

The best place to ride our carts was our driveway. It was steep and I crashed the first time, but the heap of grass cuttings cushioned my landing. I'd practice until I was as good as the best, braver, sometimes faster.

But when I was nine I learnt I wasn't really one of the boys. One Saturday, my family went down to Bobbin Head for a dip in the river. There was a picnic spot and toilets and change rooms marked MEN and WOMEN. Mum didn't want to go for a swim, so I went with Dad to change.

'She can't go in there,' Mum said.

'It's all right,' Dad said. 'No one's around.' He tousled my short hair.

The men's change room was empty and I slipped out of my shorts and into my trunks, then I slipped off my T-shirt and flexed my muscles. Dad looked at me, hesitated, then patted my shoulder. 'Let's go, Bill,' he said. I stalked out behind him.

At the entrance to the change room a boy was peeling paper from an ice-cream. He stood and stared at me. 'Hey,' he said. 'You're not a boy.'

I stuck out my chin and looked straight ahead.

'You've got a—chest!' he said.

I stopped and raised my fist. I wanted to punch him. I was burning, like a bursting inside me would make me choke. Dad was moving off ahead. I had to catch up. So I ran, faster and faster, but I didn't cry. Wouldn't let myself. Real boys didn't cry.

And I still won't, where I am now, just "one of the boys" in the big top-floor office.

Love in San Francisco

I'd always been crazy about chemistry. At school, it was watching those crystals form, seeing substances dissolve, even smelling rotten egg gas. Later though, I enjoyed another sort of bubbling, another sort of burning. When I moved on to organic chemistry I found it a bit flat at first. Nothing too exciting about finding out that what made leaves green was just chlorophyll. Some things you took for granted. Some things caught you out of the blue.

Like falling in love.

I'd always been prone to infatuation and a wink would set me off mooning for days. A kind word could get all sorts of expectations going, specially if the guy was good looking. Oh, I'd had my affairs all right. But they all fizzled out, usually when I lost interest, I told myself. A girl had her pride, didn't she? But the ache hurt all the same.

At the chemicals plant just out of Manchester where I got my first job in the lab, there was an assistant: he was tall and blonde, wore horn-rimmed glasses. He never knew what went on in my mind, though. So before long, I came out and said what I thought.

'I love you,' I whispered just as he was lining up test tubes.

He stopped and glared at me over his glasses. 'Well, I don't love you,' he said. 'I think you're crazy.'

You'd think I'd have learned to hold back. It wasn't as if it was my first rejection. There'd been a whole series of them ever since I was ten and had a crush on the cute boy next door. I'd run after him and stuff garden strawberries in his back pocket, not seeing how they got squashed. I even slipped a photo of myself into an invisible ink envelope and dropped it in his letterbox. Three weeks later I found the photo crumpled in the gutter in front of my house. I almost died.

I had other friends, though. The slow combustion ones. In Manchester there was a chap in stores. I can't even remember how we met. He was nice and dull and Rob was his name. He'd pack the materials they used in the labs. It was like we'd always had lunch together in the cafeteria.

He was a good friend, really. All the chemistry about him was just glass and metal. Harmless. No fizz. Even comfortable in a way. I started thinking I should forget about love. I told him about the lab assistant.

'You know, Rob, falling in love is the pits,' I said.

'You're so right,' he said.

Then I'd tell him about the other stupid things I'd done, like follow the gardener who completely ignored me.

Rob would tell me about his work, how many Bunsen burners had gone astray.

'But you're good with the beakers,' I said. 'Not a single one broken last shipment.'

Rob just smiled and went through the inventory of items that needed to be replaced. 'I can get you one to use as a vase,' he said.

'What do I need a vase for?'

'For the flowers.'

'What flowers?'

Rob didn't answer for a while, then he said. 'Don't think too much...not about love.'

'It's that damn word itself,' I said. 'It's like as soon as you say it, it all goes away.'

Rob went very quiet. 'Maybe it's not a matter of words,' he said.

'You mean you just know?'

'It's a little like chemistry, I suppose. Just have to get the right substances together.'

'Yeah,' I said.

Here and there Rob and I would go to a movie and then on to the pub for a drink. We'd talk about the film we'd just seen, but he'd never get really passionate about the actors the way I did.

'They're just playing roles,' he said. 'It's not real life.'

'You mean real life is like greening grass? You don't really notice?' I thought of the gardener.

Rob nodded and paid for my drink. He walked me home and at my front door he said simply, as he always did, 'See you tomorrow.'

When the budget cuts started making themselves felt at the plant, I was moved into archives and put in charge of a staff of three. It was all so new and I threw myself into my duties.

'Doesn't give me a mind for anything else much,' I said to Rob.

'It's just the beginning,' he said. 'You'll get used to it.'

He was right. I was starting to feel comfortable in the archives. There was a certain routine to being surrounded by papers. They were all about chemicals still, yet not the real thing.

But things changed with the cuts and all the supervisors had to attend management courses. The company started picking up management buzzwords and in September it also picked up a management expert. An American called Brad O'Reilly.

Brad O'Reilly was a sort of..."facilitator", he called it. I was signed up for a two-week course and soon my group was running through exercises on setting objectives, listening and "what do you propose" role games. I no longer thought much about problems in managing my team of three and felt it was still best to say what I thought. We weren't in kindergarten, after all. But the buzzwords had taken over and I started to think it was all a little pseudo, like one of those courses on interacting with others, finding oneself.

I don't really know how it happened. I certainly didn't initiate anything. One day in the cafeteria, Brad O'Reilly came towards my table. I didn't notice at first, my mind miles away. The course breaks didn't coincide with Rob's lunch break so I'd decided to eat alone for the two weeks. I even decided I'd like doing more things on my own, maybe even go to a film by myself in the evening, although I had to admit I did enjoy Rob being around. 'But I wouldn't mind being a hermit. Who needs the world?' I said to myself as I tucked into my plate of spaghetti, twiddling the fork the way I'd seen Sophia Loren do it in *Yesterday, Today and Tomorrow*.

'So how's the course shaping up for you?' Brad said as he sat down opposite me with his tray.

I shrugged. 'I don't really see anything new. It's basically common sense, isn't it?'

'Well, I hope I'm teaching you something that will help,' he said and smiled at me in a confident way. 'Maybe you can tell me what it is you don't like?'

I put my fork down and chewed slowly. He was asking me directly. The noodles tasted full. I licked my lips and swallowed. It didn't escape him.

'Well it seems like manipulation,' I said. 'I mean, can't you just say what you think.' The words tumbled from my mouth. 'For me that's the easiest way and I can hear loud and clear what's going on.'

'What sounds like manipulation?' Brad asked gently.

'All that business about pretending to listen, and then doing your own thing anyway.'

Brad sighed. 'You have to learn to step back. If you can build up some trust, then there's no manipulation.'

'It's all words,' I said. 'You don't know who really means what they say with those tricks.'

'Ever tried listening to the universe?' Brad said 'Try and see what's happening? Really happening?'

'Now it's New Age stuff, is it?' I said with a grin.

'You should have a look at the Tao sometime,' he said. 'Works for management, and for...life.'

He finished his meal. I hadn't even noticed what he'd had. My eyebrows were still raised as he walked towards the door.

The Tao, the Tao. The bloody Tao. I leafed through the pocket-sized *Tao of Management*. I can't work it out. It's just not that simple.

I'd sit at coffee and Brad would come over and go through what we'd been learning in the course. I could see how he expected me to listen, but always asking what the other person felt first, not allowing myself to say what I wanted, seemed sort of false. What I liked about him, though, was that he seemed just like Rob, in a way. No chemistry.

'Anyway, if everyone knows all the tricks, it's just moving up to another level. Guess it's OK, if you know the rules,' I said.

'So what happens if someone says to you, don't spill the milk?' Brad said one day.

'No-one's ever said that to me.'

'Just an example. Chances are you'll spill it.'

'That's a very useful hint, I must say,' I said. He was getting to me and I had to laugh.

Brad shook his head and smiled at me gently. 'And if I said: Don't think of sex?' he said suddenly.

A warmth that must have been glowing red rushed up my neck. 'Why should I think of sex?' I retorted and crossed my legs under the table.

'I'm not saying you should, I'm just saying that when someone says not to, it's easier to do than when someone says do it.'

'Do what?' I said.

'Was just an example.'

I'd meet Brad at every break and we'd lunch every day and have long discussions. Soon I began seeing him in a different way. Be objective, I said to myself. He was the sort of guy you'd never notice in a crowd—medium everything. So why do I feel nervous when we go up for coffee? Of course, I tried not to show I was nervous and I'd chatter away, not letting him get a word in. He'd just sit there and smile at me and wait for me to finish.

'So, can you see what's happening?' he said two weeks later. His eyes held mine for that split second too long and I knew I had to break off.

'I don't know,' I said quietly. The buzz of the cafeteria drifted into what seemed like a cloak of felt enveloping just the two of us. 'A four-letter word?'

'Yes.'

'Should have thought so,' I said.

'Can't you see what's happening?' he said again.

'No.' My heart was beating fast now.

'Scared to say it?'

I nodded and looked away.

'Not hard,' Brad said. 'When you mean it.'

I felt my face getting red again. How I hated those things I couldn't control.

'Think it wears out when you say it?'

I shrugged.

'Say it after me...' His smile was gentle. 'Love.'

'I can't,' I said.

'Don't say it,' he said.

Love. The word sang inside me. 'I really can't. It'll break.'

Brad touched my fingertip, just a touch, like an eyelash against a cheek.

'When's your birthday?' he said.

'March.'

'Aries?'

I nodded. 'And yours?'

'Same month.'

He seemed so quietly in control.

I hesitated. 'Pisces?' I said.

He nodded slowly.

'Well you know that Aries and Pisces just don't get on...'

'That so?' he said. His eyes ran all over my face.

'Yes. My father's a Pisces. We never got on. Water puts out the fire...'

'In rare cases...it can be nirvana.'

I swallowed and looked away.

'Don't believe it as you hear it,' Brad said. 'Just listen and trust in the universe.'

'Oh, you and your universe!'

'It doesn't mean you don't decide,' he said. 'Read the Tao yet?'

'No. Not all of it.'

'You should,' he said.

Brad's contract expired and he had to go home. 'Back to San Francisco,' he said. 'If you're ever out that way, or close by...'

'Doubt it,' I said.

We hugged in the way people do after having spent a short time with what they think are like minds.

'Try and study the Tao,' he said as he waved good-bye.

When I got back to work the next Monday, there was a message on my answer phone. I felt an unexpected yet familiar thrill as I picked up the receiver and pressed the button.

'Welcome back. Are we meeting for lunch?'

I put the receiver back in its cradle and slumped down in my chair. Then I picked it up again and dialled. 'Hi Rob. Thanks for your message. Lunch as usual would be fine.' I played back the message. My voice sounded flat.

Rob pulled out my chair in the cafeteria. 'You OK?' he said. 'How was the course?'

'Ever heard of the Tao?' I said.

Rob shook his head.

At Christmas, I sent Brad a card. He didn't send one back. In January I rang him to say that in April work would take me to a library conference in Portland.

'Portland, Maine?' Brad said.

'Portland, Oregon.'

'The city that always works,' Brad said.

'Thought that was San Francisco.'

'San Francisco works, too,' he said.

'I can't get away, but thought maybe you could come. It's only an hour,' I said. My voice felt shaky. I hoped he couldn't pick it up.

'I know,' he said. 'I'll see what I can do. Take care.'

He promised to keep in touch. I took it literally.

In March, I sent Brad a birthday card.

On my birthday, small salmon roses came to my office. My hands trembled as I opened the card. 'Happy Birthday,' it said. 'Love, Rob xxx.'

It was mid April and I was standing in the airport lounge at Portland, Oregon, scanning the incoming flights. I'd switched shift and had arranged the day off. I'd arrived early at the airport, fearing the bus would break down on the way—a silly thing, impossible in America, I thought. United Airlines flight 2122 from San Francisco was due in at 10:12. I roamed the lobby, keeping an eye on the TV set with the flight details. Then a big C. Flight 2122 cancelled due to technical difficulties. I just stood there. My knees felt all wobbly. Then I went to a pay phone and dialled Brad.

The airport bus took ages to come and the ride back to the hotel seemed so terribly long. I went up to my room and saw the red roses in a vase on the table. An envelope dangled by a tinsel thread from the cellophane wrapping. I ripped it open. 'It takes more than words to spell love right.' The words were typed like on a telegram. Then there was 'signed' followed by 'Rob'.

I threw myself into the thick bed covers. 'The city that works! Plans for the future! Stuff San Francisco!' I sobbed.

Talking Cold Turkey

I t can't be true! Cynthia stared through the window as the red Alfa backed out of her best friend's driveway. The car turned and, for a moment, its high beam flooded the kitchen.

'Christ! Who's that idiot?' Cynthia's husband said, turning from the evening newspaper spread out before him on the kitchen table.

Cynthia scraped at the crust on the baking dish. Her knife grated against the glass. She shivered. 'Mark Simpson,' she said dully as the car disappeared into the drizzly November night.

'Mark?' Douglas said. 'He back?' He glanced sideways at her then turned the page and flicked his cigarette at the half-filled ashtray.

Cynthia remembered Mark's warm smile. 'How are you, Cyn? Time for a drink?' he'd said. She'd looked at her watch. 'Just, a quick one,' she'd said. Why not? she'd thought. It was good seeing him again. He'd come by often in the old days. Never married. Then he'd come round less. 'You're looking good, Cyn,' he'd said. Then he told her about Peter. How he'd seen him slip through the doorway with the young woman in the red thigh-high boots. How he'd seen Douglas, her husband, look the other way. He hadn't told her about Marion. 'Marion and Peter are splitting up,' Cynthia said.

'What's that got to do with Mark?'

Cynthia scoured steel wool in the corners of the dish.

'Cynthia!'

She turned to face her husband. Something flashed in his look, then faded as he handed her the ashtray.

'Put this in the bin, will you,' he said.

'You smoke too much. Can't you stop?'

'Can't you?'

Cynthia froze. 'What do you mean by that?'

'Nothing.' Douglas exhaled, his eyes on the blown-out smoke.

Cynthia shook the stubs into the garbage under the sink and handed him back the brown flat bowl. Ash crusted the letters, Hotel Tasco. Cynthia remembered slipping the ceramic in her handbag the day they checked out of the honeymoon hotel. Douglas had said it didn't matter. That they expected ashtrays to be pinched.

Douglas lit another cigarette. 'Marion seeing Mark?' he said quietly.

Cynthia rinsed the dish and propped it on the drainer. 'Of course not!'

'Then what makes you say she's splitting with Peter?'

'I didn't say *she* was splitting with Peter. I said *they* were splitting up!' Cynthia watched Douglas exhale. 'Peter did disappear for a couple of days.'

'Came back though. Why would they want to split up?' Douglas said. 'Unless...'

Cynthia wiped her hands on her apron. 'What are you trying to say?'

'Come on, Cyn. They've been married almost as long as we have.'

Cynthia rinsed the dish and propped it on the drainer. She hadn't noticed the years speed by. People always said that was a good sign.

But you get into a rut, Marion had said. And then Peter had disappeared. Of course, it wasn't the first time he'd stayed away for a night. But he'd always said where he'd be. Always left a number to ring. Marion never did ring. And have him think I don't trust him? she'd said.

'As long as we have. Fifteen years,' Douglas said. He stretched his legs out and inhaled deeply.

'You make a promise when you marry. And you keep it.'

'Peter didn't keep his, did he?' Cynthia said. *Did you keep yours?*

'You girls been looking for problems where there aren't any?' Douglas said and straightened his feet into his grey felt slippers.

Cynthia took the tea towel and started wiping the dish. Her right hand circled slowly, her fingers pushing into the rounded corners, trying to catch the last beads of moisture. She turned and her eyes grazed her husband's balding crown.

'They didn't talk much,' she said.

'Who didn't?'

'Marion and Peter.'

'How can you live with someone for fifteen years and not talk?'

'They didn't talk about...'

'What?'

'Oh, nothing.' Cynthia shook out the tea towel and hung it over the edge of the sink. Its weight held it firm.

'Making mountains out of molehills?' Douglas said and then sighed. 'Why do you always look for problems?' He unfolded his newspaper and, holding it up, flicked through the pages. The rustle was deafening. 'There's an ad here about getting rid of moles from the garden. Smoke bombs. Could try it next Spring.'

Cynthia crouched to place the dish on the bottom shelf of the cupboard. Her straight skirt rode up, stretching across her thighs. She couldn't see Douglas. He couldn't see her.

Marion had been worried sick when Peter hadn't come home the next day. This time he hadn't left a number. So Marion had called the police. They'd laughed at her. Well, they hadn't laughed out loud, she'd said. But you could hear the sniggering in their voices.

Cynthia stood up. 'Do you know where he was?' she said, wiping her hands on her apron.

Douglas turned the page without looking up. 'It's none of our business,' he said.

Cynthia stared at his slippers jiggling on the end of his feet. 'You do know, don't you.' She took off her apron and hung it on the hook behind the kitchen door.

'What *is* this?' Douglas puffed a new cigarette from the glowing butt of his unfinished one.

'He told Marion he had a blackout. Got lost. Didn't know where he was.'

'So *now* I know,' Douglas said and stood up.

'Mark Simpson saw him in town,' Cynthia said quietly.

'How do you know that?'

'Marion told me.' Cynthia took the sponge and began wiping the sink. 'Mark told her he saw Peter with you. Behind the station. At noon,' she said.

'What are you saying?' Douglas said. 'She seeing Mark?' His hand closed over the ashtray as he made to leave the kitchen.

Cynthia turned to face his back. Her mind screamed at him. *I'm saying Mark Simpson saw YOU and Peter together in the red-light area at noon. That's what I'm saying.* 'Nothing,' she said. 'Just what Marion told me.' Cynthia's heart plodded as she ran the tap and held the sponge under the icy stream. 'And, no. Marion's not seeing Mark.' Cynthia turned off the tap and wrung the sponge with both hands. 'Where were you that first day? The day Peter didn't come home?'

'Hell! I don't know! Where I always am. At lunch at Vittorio's.' He stood full face towards her. 'What is this? Third degree?'

'I'm sorry,' Cynthia said. *You lying bastard.* The words screamed in her head. *You were covering for Peter. Maybe you even went with him. Where did he go? Where did you go?* She smoothed her dark brown hair behind her ear. 'Do you want a coffee?'

Douglas stared at her, his face a mask. Then it softened. 'Sure. What's on TV tonight?'

'Don't know,' she said. As she took two cups and saucers from the cupboard, the saucers almost slipped from her hand. *Mark was seeing Marion.* 'Isn't Columbo on?' she said.

Douglas opened the paper again. 'Only re-runs. Same old thing. There's a match, though.'

The kettle whistled with a piercing pitch. Cynthia flicked off the gas. The steam clouded her glasses as she poured the boiling water into the cups. 'Sugar or sweetener?'

'Sweetener,' Douglas said. 'Two. You forgotten?'

Cynthia shrugged and dropped the tiny tablets into his cup. 'That's too much for a small cup,' she said.

'Habit,' Douglas answered and left the kitchen.

And your other habits? The ones I don't know about? The so-called lunches at Vittorio's. She'd never rung the restaurant. Why should she? Peter had been gone three whole days. And her husband knew all about it. She wanted to know.

Cynthia placed the cups on the small tin tray and carried them into the living room. Douglas had settled in to his armchair, his feet propped on a footrest. The pack of Marlboro sat next to the ashtray on the coffee table. She didn't want to know anymore. Or did she?

'Why not try?' she said as she settled on the sofa and tucked a cushion behind her back.

'Try what?'

'Quitting. Quitting smoking.'

Douglas drew deeply on his cigarette and flicked the remote control of the TV. 'If I do,' he said, 'no half measures.' He stopped flicking the remote. 'Damn!'

'What's up?'

'I'm almost out,' he said. 'And now the match.'

Cynthia drained her cup. 'Quit now.'

Douglas gave her a long sad look.

Cynthia stood up and smoothed her skirt. She walked to the hall and slipped on her red hooded coat.

'Where you going?'

She pulled her car keys from her bag. 'Out,' she said. Then the corners of her mouth turned up in a wry smile. 'Out for a pack of cigarettes.'

He blew her a long slow kiss, his eyes lingering as she closed the door.

Rain fell in splats as Cynthia revved the engine of her black Mini. She turned on the wipers and watched them flap across the windscreen. Then she switched off the ignition, sagged back in her seat and sobbed.

Apple of Paradise

'It was the tomatoes,' Peter said.

'Tomatoes?' Anna ran her hand through her curly red hair. 'Or do you mean the apple of paradise?'

Anna Franklin, English freelance translator, and her East German colleague, Peter Held, were sitting at the bar of the International Conference Centre in the Swiss city of Geneva. It was a day in September 1974, European agreement had just been reached on the free flow of information and Peter had just returned from a long weekend in his hometown.

'I am from Obersdorf, a small town in Thuringia,' Peter said. 'Only about a thousand souls.'

Anna leant forward. Peter had never mentioned any details about his hometown during the three months she'd shared an office with him. Those three months had been wired with a tension of not just getting to know a new colleague, but of wondering whether he were a spy. After all, this was the first time that East and West were working together, both sides probing how far they could go. And Peter was attractive. From what he said, he lived the grand theories espoused by Sartre, Montand and Simone Signoret: the right to work and the duty to do so, the right to education, health care and housing. A paradise without competition.

'Did you feel the difference after Geneva?' Anna asked.

He nodded slowly. 'Last Saturday, at the market in Obersdorf, I saw some tomatoes glistening in a pile. Just as I reached out to squeeze one, a fat old thing in a grey apron barked at me: 'Where do you think you are?' Without thinking, I shot back, 'Geneva'.'

Anna began to notice that tomatoes came wrapped in tight transparency, supermarket perfect—the more out of season the lighter the red, paradise diluted.

That Christmas, Peter went home to Obersdorf. He didn't return to Geneva.

Anna often wondered about him, about the love apple, the apple of paradise. Like the pale-green stalks of a young tomato plant, European cooperation was fragile and needed nurturing. Topics at the conference were arranged in 'baskets' rather than under agenda items. Much like fruit and vegetables tumbling on to freshly erected market stalls, proposals jostled each other for support.

Television antennae started sprouting the length of the border between Germany's two halves. Paradise was flaunted over the ether. It had been twelve years since eight East Germans careered their bus through the Berlin Wall.

In 1976, the Soviets clamped down. Anna saw Peter at a conference in Belgrade.

'How are you? Everything all right? Been working?' she asked.

'Yes, but only in the East. Geneva must have been too long for them.'

The next day he was gone. It was only then that Anna noticed there had been no tomatoes in the Belgrade supermarkets.

In 1984, Anna was sent to West Berlin for a four-day meeting. She phoned Peter at work.

'Can you meet me at Checkpoint Charlie on Friday night? Your side, of course.'

She took the U-Bahn. Passengers alighted at each stop to be swallowed by a grey that thickened the closer she got to her destination. Proofed against sound, the tube hurtled along beneath the Wall.

Anna surfaced at the station steps and breathed out slowly as if to expel the musty air of the underground.

The crossing was two hundred metres off and smaller than she had imagined. 'Films always exaggerate,' she said aloud.

She crossed the American side and left the bath of neon for the twilighted no-man's land.

The German Democratic Republic.

She caught her breath, as harsh shafts of yellow lit up the large grey official figure of the GDR.

'Visa. 24 hours. You must change 25 Mark,' it snapped.

Anna nodded.

'Where do you stay? You must mark the hotel.'

'Hotel...Palast,' she stammered.

'The object of your visit? Business?' it sneered. 'No maga-zines? Books?'

'Just my toothbrush.'

Without acknowledging her reply, the head hovered over her passport, then dismissed her with a dull and ink-blurred stamp. She pushed the glass door open and walked out onto the street.

The air was electric. Anna felt Peter come out from the shadows on the other side of the road.

'We'll talk at the hotel,' he said. He steered her elbow three blocks in silence and only slowed their pace when the foyer lights were in sight.

The hotel bar was brightly lit but almost empty. Cards marked 'RESERVIERT' decorated two-thirds of the tables.

'Peter, it's so good to see you,' Anna said at last.

'Hush,' he said as a waiter strode towards them and led them to a corner table, one without a card.

'I'll just leave my coat on the chair,' she whispered.

'You can't do that here,' Peter said and went to hand it with his own to the dour-faced woman behind a counter marked GARDEROBE-TOILETTEN.

'The place will soon be full, by the look of those cards,' Anna said as Peter sat down opposite her.

'No it won't. Not enough staff to handle a full room. So they say the tables are reserved.'

Before she could speak, Peter said: 'Remember those tomatoes? Well that was the province. We're in the city now.' He folded his hands on the table and stared at his long thin fingers. 'The only fruit we get are apples, red ones at Christmas if we're lucky, but usually Golden Delicious. These days they are neither, just greying yellow. They taste like flour.'

Anna shook her head slowly. 'But, Peter, all the good things we used to talk about, the big things, the important things...not apples, not tomatoes,' she trailed off. This wasn't the Peter she thought she knew, wanted to know. He hadn't even said 'Hallo'. Their only physical contact had been, not a kiss, but his steely fingers on her elbow, a rudder in the dark. In Geneva it had been easy to talk ideals with her purse and stomach full.

'Oh, Peter...' The words sank into emptiness.

He looked up and smiled at her in a sad still way then ordered two beers. They talked a while, their conversation dissolving like froth until there was nothing left to say.

'Walk me back to the border. I'd better go.'

He nodded, buttoned his coat and helped her into hers. His fingers relaxed on her elbow as they walked in silence to the border crossing. At the heavy glass door his lips brushed her forehead. 'Take care of yourself,' he said.

Like a clockwork doll Anna stepped through to face the large grey official again. A taste of felt filled her mouth.

For almost five years Anna heard nothing from Peter. In the spring of 1989 a letter arrived.

'Times are changing,' he wrote. 'I've got a telephone.'

It was months before she dared to call him and when she did their exchange was guarded.

On 9th November 1989 the Wall tumbled down. The price of tomatoes went up and the vegetable became rare at the market in Obersdorf. Peter phoned Anna. He'd found competition difficult to understand, uncomfortable to digest, he said.

'You'll soon learn. You'll soon raise your tag,' she replied. Germany had become one...almost.

Satellite dishes like oversized eggshells baubled on slated roofs above peeling slogans. New outer skins affixed with yogurt, autos, underwear collided gaudily. Anna and Peter were on the circuit again, but crossed conference lines separated their assignments.

Peter moved to a village near Bonn, about one thousand souls. He bought tomatoes at the supermarket; they glistened in rows, their skins stretched shiny. One spring day his voice came through on Anna's answer phone: 'I'm still feeling my way. But can we please try?'

On her sheltered balcony in Geneva, Anna set up a trellis on the south wall. 'It may still take time,' she thought. Then she smiled and planted the apple of paradise.

Just Lunch

S he didn't trust words, at least not those that came out of people's mouths. She trusted the ones on the page. She could keep those, turn them over, dissect them and look for their true meanings. An island lives in the sea, she thought, as she dipped into the wide waters of the web and surfed into a forum for matters literary. It was there that the young woman from Crescent Street, Montreal met a man who spoke her language; it didn't matter that he was older and that he came from Mississauga—young men had burned her and Mississauga was far enough for comfort.

They discussed stories, his and hers, and books by others, and one afternoon, for that seemed to be the best time for them both, they slipped out of the group and into email. 'How about lunch,' he wrote. She didn't answer straight away. Lunch. A meal at noontime. Daylight. Can't speak while you're eating, it would be rude. Somewhere provincial where nothing could happen. What could happen? It was just lunch.

Now, five months later, she stood at the market and surveyed the stalls. Asparagus tips? Tomatoes? Rocket? Lunch had been easy the first time.

The first time was in Windsor. He'd fetched her at the station and they went to a restaurant where the road was dug up. She'd imagined him bearded, but he was clean-shaven. Can I taste your bumble berry pie, she asked as her spoon hovered in the air. Indeed, he replied. Indeed you can. They didn't speak much, their eyes did the talking. She said she'd stay overnight. He said he couldn't, had to get back to Mississauga. It was named by the French, she said. I know, he replied and gave her a hardback, Alice Munro's *The Love of a Good Woman*. In her B&B room she devoured the stories, looking for signs.

What would she need? Chives and herbes de provence. Some good wine, red and white. Chablis? Bordeaux?
The second time was in Stratford. He was a great fan of Timothy Findley. They saw his *Elizabeth Rex* and lunched late at Pazzo's. 'Did you know Tiff

and his partner ate here? They lived upstairs.' She hadn't known. He ordered ice wine. 'The grapes are the last before the frost. That's why it's so sweet,' he said. She felt as if they were on some invisible plank, needing each other just to walk it.

Two chocolate truffles, individually wrapped, and a flask of Armagnac.

The third time was in Lincoln. They sat in a park by the Falls and picnicked on the *paté* and *baguette* she'd brought from the Crescent Street market. They hardly spoke. She gave him a story she'd downloaded. "Love's Lesson" by Edna O'Brien. A bit erotic, a bit on the side. A bit sad. As he read he stroked the inside of her wrist.

At the baker's she bought a fresh baguette; at the butcher's a small fillet of beef; at the fishmonger's two large sea urchins. She still had some sour cream.

The fourth time was in Thamesford. He'd just had his first scan. Over sashimi she read him a story she'd written. 'You're dead below the neck', he said. She couldn't speak, not then, not later when he slipped a slim book into her hands: Epictetus' *The Art of Living*; and when he said *Au revoir*, she said nothing.

She smoothed out the ivory Richelieu linen and set the table with her fine bone china, two crystal glasses, two serviettes.

The last time was London. 'Don't come,' he messaged. 'My mouth's full of sores.' She didn't answer. 'But my mind is famished; let me know what you're eating.' She hesitated and then typed back: Lunch is on me.

She lit a scented white candle and placed it into a silver holder.

She would tell him about the lunch she'd prepared, the meal that they'd had. How she'd scooped the soft flesh of the sea urchins and fed him gently. How he'd sipped the Chablis and sucked on grape tomatoes and asparagus tips. How the beef had been rare and had melted like butter. (He'd passed on the Bordeaux and she'd let it be.) How she'd unwrapped the truffles and poured him a tear of Armagnac. How they'd listened for rain, but it had stayed fine. She would tell him how much he'd enjoyed it, how he'd noticed the scent of frangipani, and how he'd stayed on for dinner.

It was only much later alone in her bed, when her fingers had ceased thrusting, that she gave in and finally let herself cry.

Rites of Passion

Prague Castle was packed. The Czech President sat serene in the front row of the audience, his second wife to his right, holding his hand. On the podium, too, was Gorbachov, now solo, his Raisa lost despite the wonders of West German clinics. And then there was Bush, his Barbara sedate in her pearls, ever proud of her white hair and, with her George, confident that the strain would endure. Gorby and George were not alone, I saw, as I watched the TV. Their chests were sashed in the red and white moiré bestowed by the Czech President, a gift from the Republic, on all the architects of Freedom, ten years since the fall of the Berlin Wall.

No, I thought, they were not alone. It was the 9th of November 1999, a date laden with meaning for a nation, the world, and for individuals who had never thought further than their immediate dreams. I sipped at my glass of black-label whisky. It was 12:30 am. The family was now sleeping and the house was calm, calm enough.

Lech Walesa sat red-faced from gout and spoke his thanks to the Virgin Mary, his black madonna. Mitterand was dead, but Danielle, devoid of the red and white ceremonial sash, spoke of her François and his contribution to the edifice of future generations, knowing full well that beyond the borders of the discretion of her own country the world's mind now meandered to musings about her husband's mistress and his secret daughter. Maggie Thatcher, ever the lady, quoted Byron and later cocked her eternally coiffed head at the strains of the syncopated viola.

I had to agree with her for once. The music was weird. Yet the strains of a gypsy-like wail trying to find its place in a structure hardly freed from the constraints of classicism, spoke to me. And then the camera zoomed in on Vaclav. I had always found him attractive and now I wondered whether it had only been because of his dreams.

Vaclav Havel smiled as he held the hand of his ex-actress wife. He had lost a lung, but gave the impression that as a re-born non-smoker he was feeling pretty good and that he had managed to bring together the things he had wanted to say in his writing, despite having to endure the constraints of his office. Then came Kohl. Helmut Kohl. I leaned forward to listen. What was it he said? Of course he should know. Freedom did not necessarily mean that one was free.

I turned off the TV and went to the bedroom. My husband was snoring, gently. His blanket had slipped, baring a hip, so I tucked him in, my lips brushing his forehead as I withdrew. He did not stir as I slipped under the covers by his side.

It had been a rough day, the 9th of November. I should have expected it, had I had any thoughts for the tricks history can play. The evening before, he'd been rushed to hospital. We live out in the country so couldn't take chances. The ambulance was out, so the fire brigade came. He'd had a seizure. His heart was breaking. Two hours later I raced with my daughter to the hospital. No point in coming earlier, they'd said. It will be all right. And so the same night we brought him back home.

Our daughter is sixteen. She was conceived in East Germany, the German Democratic Republic then. My husband and I had gone over to see friends we had met on a previous trip, friends who couldn't get out. We were brave then. It was easy to be brave and there was a certain romance in defying the Wall. We were firm, we from the West. What did we have to lose? Is it true that our heroes had no one at stake, nothing to lose but their own face?

We used to send our friends, Gerd and Helga, Swissair and Lufthansa timetables. They'd sit at breakfast, they said, with photo books open on the table showing the cities they wanted to visit.

'Flight 241 to Paris is ready for takeoff,' Gerd said. He always played pilot.

'He needs to assert himself,' Helga said. 'He's a plumber. I'm a judge. Everything is equal in the GDR of course. And gender is almost more equal than our ideology.' We all laughed at that.

'We don't speak to others about our dreams,' Gerd said. I had the distinct feeling that his gaze grazed my cheek. 'Thank you so much for the timetables,' he added.

Ten years ago, Gerd and Helga must have been having their first real champagne flight, their last simulation. When the Wall came down, they went to Paris. It wasn't as they'd imagined, they'd scribbled on a postcard of the Eiffel Tower. Who would have thought that that metal construction would be for eternity. It had never been intended that way. So unlike the Wall, I remember thinking. We had hoped to see Gerd and Helga in Paris, but somehow we missed them by a day or two. They had become just like anyone else. We have not seen or heard from them since. Seeing Prague Castle though, brought it all back and I wondered what they were doing right now.

Despite having gone to bed after midnight I rose early the next morning. Our daughter was already up and dressing as I came in to kiss her good morning. She was wearing her Calvin Klein bra, the one like mine that we'd bought together in the US last year. Just down from her neck I noticed a love bite. I hugged her and as I drew back I mentioned the bite. She laughed.

'I love you,' I said.

'Me too,' she answered.

(My daughter tells me about her friends. Their problems. Her best friend is seeing a shrink.)

'She keeps dropping guys straight after she hooks them,' she said.

'Shrink?'

My daughter nodded. 'Her mother doesn't understand,' she said.

The love bite just down from my daughter's neck is in the shape of a heart. 'Is your period on time?' I asked.

She nodded.

'Don't tell your father,' I said.

'About the love bite?'

'No.'

'Oh,' she said. 'I already have.'

'Why?'

'He asked me. I told him.'

'When?'

'Yesterday.'

'When?'

'After school.'

'Where?'

'When Pierre dropped me off at the corner.'

'Why?'

'Someone in the village made a comment about Pierre and me.'

I hoped she couldn't hear my heart wings flutter as colour crept up my throat and for a split second I felt what my husband must have when they rushed him to hospital, when he'd realised that his daughter no longer was just his little girl.

Gerd and Helga never had children. Helga was barren, Gerd told me a long time ago. 'And anyway,' Gerd added, 'I wouldn't want a child that couldn't be free.' They have their freedom now. It's a free for all.

Just before his seizure, just before the pain in his gut punched all air away my husband accused me of having a lover. He'd found a phone number and name scrawled on the back of the cleaning woman's weekly bill.

'Ring the number,' I'd said.

'No.'

My husband is still sleeping soundly, or perhaps he has woken and is just dozing. Our daughter has already left for school. The 9th of November is now history.

I go to the bathroom and look in the mirror and a blur of faces looks back at me. As I focus the face of a woman stares at me. I know her like no one else really does. The mirror woman's mascara is smudged; she must have forgotten to clean up before bed. I rummage in the back of the cupboard and look for some make-up remover. How can you remember not having done or said something? How can you forget games the wild card plays?

Matthew

I didn't know my son was born until the day after. I didn't know if I'd even wake up. It was three days before I dared go up to his room. From the first day, Jack had gone to the room our baby shared with ten others like him in the intensive care section of the maternity ward, but I couldn't do it straight away

'It's over 30 degrees,' the nurse said. 'We can take them out for a bit. It's warmer in here than in the incubators.'

It was clammy in the August heat as I watched through the paned door. I didn't know which baby was mine. I couldn't hear any of them crying. But the one closest to where I was standing scrunched its closed eyes, stretched out its froglike legs and opened its tiny mouth in a soundless wail. My breasts wept.

I stared as the limp body drew its legs up, then rolled over to one side. A white capillary of milk ran into its nostrils. The nurse looked over to me; she held up five fingers and pointed to the small round watch pinned to her breast pocket. I nodded dully. I watched as she slipped each tiny body back into its Plexiglas box. Then she waved me in and pointed to the incubator by the door.

'You can touch him,' she said.

I eased my hand through the hole in the side of the box and with an unsteady finger stroked the down on my son's head.

'He'll be in here till he doubles his weight,' the nurse said.

And till I heal, I thought, clasping the drip holder that I dragged with me. Maybe longer.

'Come often,' she said. 'Your husband comes every day.'

I nodded and said, 'I know.' Then left.

It was all meant to have been so different. After the age it took to get pregnant. Sex more than just pleasure. Sex with a reason. The contortions, the full moon, the food—alkaline, acidic—the gyrations. How we laughed with my legs up on the door of the cupboard next to our bed. We'd tried it all. The thermometer, the stopwatch, timed to ovulation. Then, after we gave up, it happened.

I loved being pregnant. I was never sick. I spent all my money on parenting magazines, read all the books. Jack even quit smoking. Why, I was going to have my baby, our baby. I might even have him squatting in the garden, maybe underwater, like those Russian women. It was all just so perfect. I grew rounder and rounder and everywhere I went I saw women like me—full, juicy, fertile. I sank my teeth into dripping figs and salty fat gherkins and thick oozing cheese. My baby would tickle my insides with the flutter of butterfly wings and I bathed in Jack's gaze.

My mind drifted to our first meeting in Cannes ten years earlier. The blue sky. The blue water. The sun. The red and white striped umbrellas. I craved aphrodisiacs.

'Let's take a week in Cannes,' I said. 'Share some of that sunshine? We can eat oysters again.'

'You and your oysters,' Jack said and tousled my hair.

'Please, let's go.'

'The Med's not the place anymore. Too much slick. Too filthy.'

'The Atlantic, then?'

'Brittany? It's colder.'

'Don't care,' I said. 'The oysters are fresh every day.'

Jack stroked my belly. 'Won't gherkins do?'

I wriggled under his touch. 'No,' I said. Then I smiled at him tenderly. I was in my sixth month.

Jack and I hadn't wanted a baby straight away. There were so many things we had wanted to do. Wanted to explore. Not that we did all we had wanted, though. Then out of nowhere it was time and we both knew it.

We booked a week in La Baule on the bracing Brittany coast. We ate oysters. Fresher than fresh. It was heaven.

When we got back to Geneva I was rested and bright. Jack went with me for my checkup. He covered my hands with his as they rested on my belly while we sat waiting for my turn.

Then Dr Lafont called me in. Jack stayed behind. Dr Lafont took my blood pressure.

'We'll have to keep you in hospital,' he said. 'Do some tests.'

'But I'm perfect! I feel great!' I said.

'It's for your baby.' Then he called Jack in. 'It may be toxoplasmosis.'

Toxoplasmosis? It can't be. Oh, sure, I'd read about avoiding raw meat, and we didn't even have a cat. It was all in the magazines.

'She may not go to term,' Dr Lafont said.

Suddenly I thought of the oysters, of a colleague who wouldn't touch them. 'It's not because of my religion,' he'd said. 'My friend died. They're filthy.' How could I have forgotten. I thought of my mother. 'Only ever eat oysters at the seaside,' she'd always said.

'Take her straight to the maternity ward,' Dr Lafont said to Jack.

They put me in a room by myself. In the first week, several times a day, the nurse would prod my belly with a wooden trumpet, like a primitive hearing aid, to listen for the baby's heartbeat. A few days later they hitched me up to technology and when I woke every morning the quiet red blinking would tell me we'd gained another day. Then they'd spike my belly daily with cortisone jabs.

'To speed the baby's development,' the nurse said.

I raised my eyebrows.

'The lungs. Once the lungs are OK.... Now get some rest.'

I had never rested so much in my life. I was flat on my back all the time. I was trapped and my baby was trapped inside me.

Well-meaning friends would tell stories about siblings born into cotton-wool cushioned shoeboxes. How they were stronger than all the rest. How they were survivors. 'You'll see,' they said. I didn't believe them.

The magazines spoke of the wonders of childbirth, the attendant fathers, the bonding, the love.

'It's not your fault,' Jack said. 'We didn't know.'

'We should have known. Dammit!' All those magazines and perfect worlds. Why hadn't I remembered my colleague's words? God had his laws. They were laws of hygiene. Why hadn't I believed him?

When I was at 32 weeks, Dr Lafont said, 'We can't wait much longer.'

Jack was home mowing the lawn when they rang him. 'She'll be in theatre at six this evening,' the nurse said to him on the phone.

I went in alone. I wasn't scared. Somehow I'd stepped outside of it all—the baby, Jack, outside of my life.

When I came to, Jack was by my side. 'Thank God you're OK.'

'Did you see the baby?' I said.

'No.'

My voice caught in my throat. 'But they must have passed you from the theatre...'

'A trolley raced by. An aluminium bundle,' Jack said and stared at me. 'That was our baby?'

'They say it's a boy,' I said as tears ran down my cheeks.

Jack didn't cry, but his eyes were watery. 'Our son,' he whispered and kissed my forehead.

'I'm scared,' I said.

'So am I,' he said.

We sat in silence, his hand wiping my cheek.

'The main thing is you're all right,' he said. 'Do you want to see him?'

I shook my head. The tears wouldn't stop.

'Take your time,' Jack said.

Our son weighed one kilo at birth. Jack had weighed five and now weighed one hundred.

When they took off my drip, Matthew was still in the incubator.

On the day I left hospital they moved Matthew into a room full of cots. I would come in each day and learn how to change him. I'd bathe him in a washbasin, so small was he.

'I'm frightened I'll drop him,' I said.

'They bounce,' the nurse said. 'Don't worry. Babies are tough.'

Yes, Matthew was tough. He was so tough that I felt he didn't need me. He refused my breast. He'd become used to the liquids dripping directly into him through a tube so I'd pump my milk for him to have in the bottle.

'You're not trying hard enough,' the ward nurse said. 'You don't really want to breast feed.'

'I want to, I want to,' I said. 'It's just that he doesn't. He cries.'

'He feels you don't want to.'

Matthew had to stay two months in hospital, the two months that I couldn't keep him inside me. I'd healed on the outside, but I'd cry every night. Jack would hold me.

When Matthew came home, I wanted to hold him. I picked him up and he cried. I gave him to Jack and watched as my husband settled down on the couch, our baby splayed over his belly, contented. Soon both were sleeping.

When Matthew was three months old he began to fill out the baby clothes I had bought for our newborn. Jack fed him and rocked him. I went back to work. I missed Matthew, but he didn't want me. What was I to think when he cried when he saw me?

'I've failed as a mother,' I said to Jack one night.

Jack cradled my face with his hands. 'You're just trying too hard. Don't think ahead,' he said. 'Thank God for each day.'

'It's not God,' I said.

Jack stroked the hair from my face. 'One day at a time,' he said. Then he drew me close and rocked me. 'Let's bring Matthew in with us. Lay him between us.'

I pulled back. 'I'll roll onto him. Squash him.'

'You won't,' Jack said and kissed me.

That night the fever came. We woke to the hot twitching of Matthew's body.

'Strip him down,' Jack said.

I was about to protest, but Jack had already gone to phone the hospital. He called from the hall: 'They said strip him down.'

I held the naked baby against me as we drove through the dead town. The hospital lights glowed yellow. We rushed through the entrance. Matthew convulsed again. Then he was still.

Jack went home at three and I stayed through the night by Matthew's bedside, just watching him breathe. With the first light of day our son opened his eyes. I swore he was smiling at me.

'Take him,' the nurse said.

I held my son close, held him and held him. He snuggled against me and sighed into sleep. All was quiet and warm. I was still standing there with Matthew in my arms when Jack arrived an hour later.

'One day at a time?' I said.

Jack nodded. Then he took us both in his arms.

The Caravan

Paul was just three weeks old when we brought him home from the orphanage that sunny spring Sunday. Bells were ringing all around—church bells and doorbells, and the phone never stopped.

We'd just got the flat. You had to have at least two rooms, and we had three, not counting the kitchen. We were the right age and had just enough income with two salaries. I knew everything would work out even though Marsha had to promise to work only part time once the baby came. I'd get a Saturday job.

In the beginning, the social assistant came by once a month to see that everything was going as planned. When Paul turned two, she came every three months. She only came once when he was three. Then we were on our own.

One summer Sunday we were out strolling Paul and had gone down by farmer Grobet's when we saw the caravan. It was round and sunny yellow, squatting in the field in the midst of poppies, daisies and cornflowers.

'Do you think we could?' Marsha asked.

'You mean rent it?'

She lifted Paul from the stroller and, holding him belly to belly, she looked up at me, nodding. Her smile said it all and I had to smile, too. I looked towards the caravan sparkling yellow in the sunshine. It may have been the haze, but it too seemed to be nodding.

'Just in the summer,' Marsha said. 'It'll be good for Paul.'

Farmer Grobet rented us the caravan for 200 francs a year. We had to look after it, he said as he poured us fresh cider to toast the deal. Like my job as a clerk at the local *Mairie*, the flat was for weekdays, but on Saturdays I'd come home to the caravan after selling brooms at the nearby market.

Marsha pegged up blue gingham curtains and I freshened the paint around the windows and mowed arcs around the front step so that Paul could play and still be kept in sight. We didn't have much money, but we always had flowers. Old coffee jars made good vases for the cornflowers and daisies, but not the poppies.

'Poppies wilt,' Marsha said. 'They're better off in the ground.'

When Paul started kindergarten, Marsha took in mending work. She'd bring it to the caravan and sit stitching in the sunshine. I had my own stand of brushes at the St Julien market. It was good to be back in the town of my birth and I'd call out to the shoppers to try my curved brushes, the ones for the tartar, to make their taps gleam.

In the Indian summer of Paul's tenth birthday, Marsha became listless. We were out at the caravan and she wiped away at the dull stainless steel sink. It had been weeks since she'd washed the curtains and they were starting to droop. We'd always had to lug the barrels of water for rinsing, but all of a sudden they began to feel heavier.

'I'm homesick,' Marsha said as she wiped over the windowsill.

'Isn't this home? Aren't you happy in St Julien?'

She shrugged.

'But you wanted to come to France. Be with me.'

'Can't we go back?'

'My home's here, Marsha. So is Paul's.'

Her eyes gazed at me flatly.

'St Julien's your home, too, now.'

She nodded. I took it as her acceptance of my truth.

When Paul was twelve, Marsha went back to work fulltime in the local supermarket. She began spending more time there. More time than with Paul. When he was thirteen, she moved into accounts. Then her career took off.

We were out at the caravan. It was the end of the summer and Marsha was stacking the dishes. Paul was outside. We watched him through the window. He circled us in larger and longer arcs. Marsha wiped the last glasses as she gazed after him.

'He's your son, too, Marsha,' I said.

She poured cold water into the basin. 'Is he?' she answered. Her voice was flat. 'He doesn't think so.'

'But we had to tell him,' I said. I propped my back against the door. I could see Paul spiral away.

'We?'

'All right. I.'

'Why did you do it? He feels a loss. He can't understand he's an orphan.'

'They said he had to know.'

'But not out of the blue. Just because you were mad with me.' She folded the tea towel. It was wet. It fell to the sink with a slap. 'We should have told him earlier. Quietly.'

'Marsha. We were scared.'

She drew away.

'I was scared.' I could barely hear myself say it.

Marsha shook her head slowly. 'I'll never be his mother now,' she said.

Through the window I saw Paul's circles close in on us in the dusk. I took Marsha by the shoulders. Steadied her. My gaze bore into hers. She broke away. Paul's face was blank as he opened the door.

It was late in the autumn in the year of the big rain. Paul was fourteen and winds whipped through the field. This time Marsha hadn't been with us out at the caravan. When we came home she looked distracted. Her grey suitcase sat open on the bed. 'I'm going home,' she said.

Paul and I stayed in the flat. He didn't say much. At Easter he asked if he could go off on a trip with his mates. I thought it would do him good and slapped him on the shoulder—like a man.

When he left he was wearing his Iron Maiden T-Shirt.

The flat felt so empty I went out to the caravan. It was like a shell curving in on me so I got out my brushes to get rid of the cobwebs. It wasn't long before I had things spruced up again. But I left the coffee jars empty.

Late on Sunday the police contacted me at the caravan. They'd been trying to find me for 36 hours. Paul was in a clinic in Zurich. An overdose. He'd been lucky.

It was autumn again when Paul and I went back to the caravan, but something was different. For the first time I realised it was more than the dust and the cobwebs. The paint needed attention. Paul was quiet.

We never spoke about Zurich. In October I suggested the caravan again. Paul said no. In November, Marsha phoned. I said how things were. 'Be careful,' she said.

I bought Paul a motorbike for Christmas. All winter he polished it. He was sixteen. In the Spring he went off for odd days here and there, then one weekend he stayed away. His school marks had started slipping. I tried to talk to him about it, but he just stared and said nothing. I suggested the caravan, a change of scenery. He shook his head and plugged rock in his ears.

His lips mouthed the word 'poppy.' That night he went out.

The police phoned me at five the very next morning. This time he hadn't been lucky.

In mid-summer I lost my job at the *Mairie* and I had to leave the flat. I still had my stand at the market and the old caravan. It was all I had left.

The August sun was lost behind distant clouds as I came through the field. The caravan was dirty mustard now. It looked like it was sinking in weeds.

I could feel the rub of black clouds knotting behind me. I swung my case of brushes from the boot. I had them all there, the short ones—for the easy corners. The telescopic ones for the cobwebs. I never said they couldn't go round corners, or that you missed the simple bits right up close. Everyone had cobwebs, didn't they?

There was something about the place that I'd never really noticed before—its flatness, the small matt windows, the way it rounded its back—its bald and grubby flesh exposed. I wanted to turn back, but I was already more than halfway there.

A single path to the door had crushed the grass, stiff and brown from drought. Stubble spiked through my trousers, but I brushed it aside. A black square in the distance now waved slowly in the heavy air. Just like washing—hung out to dry.

I strode ahead. A splat of rain caught me on the shoulder. Then another. My feet slithered as drops pelted down on stalks long past saving. The black Iron Maiden T-Shirt clamped into the top of the window flapped dully then stuck against the pane. Rust gnawed through the duco blistering around the window edges.

I peered in the other window. Water dribbled down the walls into veins of wet cobwebs. I sank to the gridiron step at the door and let the rain beat down upon me.

The Boy from Bul

In late Spring 2000, I spent almost three weeks in Istanbul, taking notes for my boss at a UN conference on communications; delegates and staff numbered almost three thousand. We were shuttled from the airport to our hotel behind the noisy hub of Taksim Square and then straight on to the newly completed Rumeli Building. It had been erected in the same swift way Sultan Mehmet must have built the Rumeli Fortress in preparation for the final attack on the city that led to the fall of the Byzantine Empire.

After a week of day and night meetings, I wanted a Sunday by the sea, away from anyone that I knew. I took a bus over the Galata Bridge up to the Blue Mosque and walked down the hill to the docks. It was three p.m., and I was hungry. Since arriving in Istanbul, I'd worked my way through a diet of spicy kebabs, but now I had a craving for fish. Fresh from the sea. Grilled. The only condiment, a slice of lemon.

A string of restaurants bordered the waterfront. I stopped at the first and sat down at a table by the deserted walkway. The waiter showed me a platter of raw fish. I picked one, ordered white wine.

At the next table sat a young woman with her young husband. A scarf shielded half of her forehead, but her nipples strained through her bra, firmly outlined against her white Lycra top. She resembled a photo I had seen of Harem women, bare-breasted but clothed everywhere else from neck to knee.

When I finished my fish and a half litre of wine, the waiter told me his name was Murat. I told him that I was working in Istanbul. He said he had worked in Germany for three years and was glad to be back home. He pointed across the sea. 'I like working in Europe and living in Asia,' he said. He had been married just one year.

'Does your wife wear a scarf?' I asked and glanced in the direction of the young woman.

Murat shook his head.

'Do you drink alcohol?'

'No,' he said.

'Your religion?'

'One day a friend put an aspirin in my Raki. Never again.'

'Do you smoke?' I said, imagining Harem women with water pipes.

Murat shook his head. 'It tastes foul.'

The contrasts in this city were getting to me. The noise and pollution of Taksim Square and its arteries were worlds away from the breezes of a boat trip on the Bosphorus. The palaces, once homes to sultans, were tourist attractions showcasing opulence. Up past Ortaköy, just under the bridge, Istanbul's "Golden Gate" linking Europe with Asia, were the most expensive waterfront houses in the world. A few blocks from work at the Rumeli Centre were modern boutiques: Elite, Naf Naf. On the street, women with scarved heads and long coatdresses, some in blue denim, brushed against teenagers in platforms shoes and jeans, navels peeking out from beneath short T-shirts. And here in town my bus had just brought me past crumbling facades.

Istanbul was a city where street boys belly-flopped onto the low backs of cars, daring the traffic, and jumped off just before they fell. A city of more than 18 million, and I wondered how on earth they could all be counted.

'Shoes? Shoeshine?' a voice said.

I'd sensed the figure skipping up and down the walkway, but had been too caught up in my daydreaming to actually see him. I looked down at my dusty loafers and shook my head.

Murat came over and ruffled the boy's hair. 'This is Ahmed. One of our free ones.'

I raised an eyebrow and looked at the boy. He must have been about ten, but he had that wise hungry look of the street kids.

'He lives with his friends,' Murat said and pointed to two slightly taller boys on the edge of the walkway right on the waterfront. They giggled. I looked back at Ahmed. He must have been one of those who'd slipped through the census.

'Shoes dirty,' Ahmed said.

'I like them that way.'

The boy grinned and sat down by my side on the wooden box he'd been carrying. Murat served me Raki. 45 proof. 'It's on the house. You didn't finish your fruit.'

I nodded. Swore I would drink the white liquid slowly. 'No aspirin?'

Murat laughed and cleared the last plates from the table.

'Only 1.7 million Lira,' Ahmed said.

'You're joking.' I grinned at his cheek and turned back to my Raki.

'One million.'

'Come here,' I said. 'Do you go to school?'

'Shoes?'

'School.'

'Don't have school. Shoes?'

'You speak English.'

'English. *Danke schön. Voulez-vous? Gracias. Amore.*'

I called Murat over. 'He should learn to read,' I said.

Murat said something to Ahmed and the boy fired words back at him. 'He *can* read,' the waiter said.

I held out a Bic.

Ahmed shrugged. 'Shoes?'

I sighed. 'Try.' I gave him 700,000 Lira. 'Keep the secret,' I said. 'Show me how you write.'

Ahmed grinned and pocketed the bills. His friends were watching, egging him on. He turned to them and puffed out his small chest.

'English,' I said.

'Thank you very much.'

'Thank you very much is not enough. I can say *Teşekkür ederim*, too.'

Ahmed grabbed the pen. Drew squiggles and dots.

'Murat?'

'He has written in Turkish.'

'What did he write?'

'I don't understand.'

'You don't understand?' I said.

'He wrote that he did not understand.' Now it was Murat's turn to sigh.

Ahmed wrote again.

'Murat?'

'I want to come to your country with you.'

'He wrote that?' I asked.

Ahmed was smiling. In the background his friends were doubling up with laughter. 'Learn English,' I said, feeling suddenly foolish.

He grinned again and then skipped off with his shoebox. His friends hugged him and the three of them slouched down the walkway, Ahmed in the middle, his friends' arms over his shoulders. He was a hero. And my shoes were clean.

I sipped the rest of my Raki and looked out on the Samara Sea towards Asia. A rusty tanker skimmed close by the shore, its Plimsoll line hidden by oily water.

The next Friday, my husband flew in for the weekend to accompany me home. On Sunday, I wanted to take him to the restaurant by the sea. Have him meet Murat and Ahmed. Even let him see the young wife with her proud breasts defying her headscarf.

I hailed a taxi on the road up to Taksim. We had to cross over one lane. I stepped from the footpath, but my husband pulled me back.

I pulled away, holding his hand. 'Eye contact,' I said. 'Just see who backs down first.'

We got in the taxi, and he blew air through his lips. 'Dangerous sport. You cross like a local.'

I shrugged, feeling strangely proud of myself on my last weekend in Istanbul.

The old, black taxi careened down winding roads and past crumbling buildings. The Galata Bridge was strangled with carts and cars.

'Restaurant,' I said to the driver. 'Down by the sea. The docks.'

We seemed to be going in circles, and I had lost all sense of direction. 'The docks. Water.' My navigation skills had obviously irritated the driver, and he suddenly stopped by the side of a pier.

'We'd better get out,' I said. 'It's not far. We can walk.'

My husband did not say a word.

The sun was hot, and we walked, the restaurant now a mirage in my mind. 'It's just round the next corner,' I said.

'Let's go back. There's nothing this way.'

'We're almost there. Just one more corner.'

And there they were, the restaurants, one after the other. The walkway by the sea. The fish, fresh in their baskets, almost spilling onto the street. I looked for Murat. He wasn't there.

'Let's eat,' said my husband.

'Not here,' I said. 'There.'

'Where?'

'I don't know anymore. I can't remember.'

We were tired and hungry. We must have walked about five kilometers in the hot sun. It was 3 p.m. We went to the nearest table and sat down. Ordered fish. Ate. Drank wine. It was not the same as the Sunday before.

Then I saw Ahmed. He held a rose. I caught his eye. He looked at me as if I were a stranger, then stretched out the rose. I shook my head and pointed to his shoes. One toe had burst through the seams of his sneakers. They were not the same ones he had worn last time. He turned away and walked out of sight.

We were settling the bill when Ahmed came back. He was carrying his polish and wooden box. But he did not stop at our table. No tourist hassling. No recognition. I didn't know what was worse.

I reached for my husband's hand. 'I want to go home,' I said.

Mind Wisps

My name is Jason and I was spun from the strands of my true love's mind. When did imagination defy reason? I think I remember: I was on my horse, my mare Floria, behind the chemistry building. Romina's bus had pulled up. It was the day Romina started university, the day I fell in love with her. I imagined that she must smell of frangipani, if only I could have got close enough to her. But there were so many others: the tall blond youths in cut-off jeans, their feet bare because no shoes, no sandals could contain their board bumps. Their surfboards lined the outside walls of the library and there was no place for my dappled mare, even though no one could see her. Sometimes Romina's mind would call me over, tell me that, on the far lawns where the grass was still rich in the shade, there was a place for my horse to graze. But the mind wisps that shimmered in the summer heat were soon blown away by a strong sea breeze that carried Romina across worlds. And so, I lost my love before ever really having found her.

It was only much later when Romina was into the fifteenth year of her marriage that I heard her mind call me again. Floria was dead, her carcass long since transported to Arabia—as sausage fodder. I was grieving in the Sahara when a scent of frangipani beckoned. Romina was alone in a restaurant in Vienna. I knew then that I loved her, more than any living being. And we had shared the same sun. So I came.

Romina had begun doing things alone, or so it seemed to the outside. Of course, it may have started much earlier, but it was that one day, instead of waiting for her husband, instead of seeking other company, that she decided to go to a restaurant in the city and dine alone, that she called me.

'Jason,' she said. Only I saw her lips move. 'Tell me about your horse. The places you went with her.'

'You remember Floria?'

Romina nodded and sipped from her wine. 'How could I forget a mare dappled in mauve,' she said. A red pearl clung to her lower lip and her grey eyes drifted to another time, another place.

I was surprised at first that she could summon me, expect us to slip into roles we never had, ones of which I had always dreamed.

I told her how I roamed the coastline with Floria, how we followed the beaches way up north into the underskirts of the rain forest. There was shade there, but Floria needed lush plains and the expanses where she could gallop free soon became roads ripped by bitumen or parched by desert winds. One evening as the sun bled over the horizon the kangaroo bars of a speeding truck bludgeoned my mare full on. I rolled from her back into the sand embankment.

A hulking man in a dark singlet jumped from his cabin to inspect the tyres of his truck. 'Bloody pothole,' he said. I ducked my head as he shone his torch about in the dust road. Then he hoisted himself back up and drove on. Floria was dead.

'But Floria didn't disappear,' I said to Romina. 'Men came for her. Shipped her to Arabia, where her flesh was mingled with that of lambs, to be sold as sausage at the markets. Her mane and tail, those strong strands were fashioned into wisps to keep the flies away.'

'I've tasted such meat,' Romina said. 'And I've seen those wisps.' She pulled a key ring from her handbag and held out a white plait of horsehair. 'I bought it from an Arab at the market,' she said.

'But why didn't you call me then?' I said.

'I wasn't ready.'

'Were you here then? In 1968?'

Romina stared beyond me. 'Not here exactly,' she said. 'In Prague, with Jiří.'

Romina arrived in Prague the week before the Russians. The city was alive with the breath of Spring and students filled the cafés. She was drinking a Pilsen in Café Hawelka when Jiří came to her table.

'American?' he said and then gestured at the empty chair facing hers.

Romina nodded that he might sit. 'Australian,' she said.

'Tell me about Australia,' Jiří said and drew a pack of tobacco and fine papers from the pocket of his corduroy jacket.

'It's far away,' Romina said as she watched him roll a cigarette.

'That's why I want to know,' Jiří said .

Romina told him about the beaches and the bush, the rainforests soaking into mangrove swamps and thinning into the ocean.

'Come with me,' Jiří said. 'I live with three other students down below the castle.'

Romina stood. Jiří laughed and slipped an arm about her shoulder. They crossed the Charles Bridge with its statues, stopping to make a wish—a prayer, he said—as they rubbed the brass plaque, shiny from so many hands, so many hopes.

The flat was on the third floor. Books piled in crazy towers in each corner of the room. Mattresses lined the walls. No one else was there. Romina slipped into Jiří's arms and silently they made love.

'So this is the rainforest that comes to the ocean,' Jiří said closing his eyes as Romina traced a finger over the wing of his collarbone. 'I think I shall like Australia.'

Jiří took Romina through the town, past the Jewish cemetery with its stones thrown helter skelter, and on to Wenceles Square where they sat and laughed in the streetside cafés.

Two days later the tanks came. People rushed onto the broad avenue. Some were beaten back by khaki clad figures in white shiny helmets; others assembled in haphazard rows to stop the tanks, flesh against metal. Jiří stood in the first row as the tanks ploughed the bodies in their path.

'I called to you then, Jason,' Romina said.

'It was perhaps too soon,' I said. I thought of Floria, how her body had been sleek and graceful, how her long elegant legs had tensed with power, how her coat had glowed in a curious blend of—yes, Romina had seen the hues—a blend of grey and mauve.

'I fled to Vienna. It was there I met Franz.' Romina told me how Franz had tried to pluck her from the sorrow that weighed her down. When broadcasts and papers were full of the news of a young student who had set himself on fire as a protest for freedom, Franz must have thought that she had at last shut the door on her memories of Prague.

'I married Franz,' Romina said. 'The better we took for granted...'

'And the worse?' I asked.

Romina's plate was hardly touched. 'That, I thought, I had already had,' she said. 'Franz surely did. He is a good man.'

'Do you love him?' I asked.

'Yes.' Romina took another sip of wine. 'I do love Franz.' Her gaze followed the smoke of an almost extinguished cigarette in an ashtray on the next table. 'Three weeks ago, he took me to Prague. The Charles Bridge was lined with artists, students, hawkers, and their watercolours, even the photos of the city, were tinged with mauve. There was some jewellery on a stand. I saw the key ring.'

I watched as Romina fingered the strands of what might have been the mane I had gripped as Floria galloped through our dreams.

'On Wenceles Square,' she said, her voice low, 'there is a simple plot of flowers with two photo portraits. One of Jan Palach.'

'Jan Palach?' The name resonated.

'The student who set himself on fire when the Russians killed the Prague Spring. He and his friend lived in the same flat as Jiří.'

I took Romina's hand and clasped it between both of mine. 'But didn't Franz know?'

'Franz thought enough time had gone by. Perhaps it was a test, more for himself than for me. He did not know Jan had anything to do with Jiří. Didn't even know about Jiří. Just that I had seen someone die.'

I stroked her hand as if the hypnotic movement could strengthen the bond already between us.

'Franz is a good man,' she said. 'But he will never understand. Jiří wasn't just my lover, Jason. He was a time.'

'Why did you buy the key ring?' I asked softly, still stroking the back of her hand.

'I don't know,' she said. 'It was as if something was calling me, waiting for me to come.'

'Are you ready now?' I said.

No Man's Land

Dak was the only member of the family whose name did not appear on the list tacked to the door. The names of all men, women and children living in the house had to be on that list. Dak was family, Dak was a dog. It was 1957. Algeria. I was nine. SOLDIERS WERE COMING.

I tugged at my father's sleeve. 'Papa, they can't take Dak!'

'Inside! Get inside!' he said and closed the wooden louvered door. The grey sheet of paper tacked on the outside fluttered as he shut out the dusk.

My father dropped to his knees before me. He placed a square calloused hand on each of my shoulders. We were eye to eye.

I was determined. 'No Papa!'

My father's eyes drooped like his black mustache and held my tears. 'Samir. We have to hand her over. We have to.'

He rose and drew my mother close to him. My sister, Aïcha, clutched our mother's skirts and sucked her thumb. She was too young to understand.

'If Dak makes the slightest sound, we're all lost,' my father said.

'I've trained her, Papa,' I said. 'She won't make a sound.'

My father looked at my mother's upturned face, then at me, then back at her. She nodded slowly, one hand around his waist, the other stroking the top of my sister's head.

My father turned his face down once more to my mother's. 'What about Aïcha?'

'She will be all right,' my mother said. 'She knows Dak is one of the family.' And she kept stroking Aïcha's head.

I think Dak was the only dog left in our village. The soldiers had made us round them up. Then they'd take them away. In the early days we'd heard shots in the night. The soldiers feared the dogs would warn us. They would go from house to house—once, twice, sometimes three times a week, their jackboots thunk-thunking in the dust. If they heard a dog bark, they'd haul it out and shoot it. One of them would sling the carcass over his shoulder, like a goat to be readied for skinning and skewering.

But I had trained Dak to keep quiet. A tiny twitch would signal movements outside the house, but never did she make a sound, not even when she was huddled under carpets and swathes of sheeting.

That day, the soldiers rapped on the door and barged past my father. They kicked cushions and carpets aside and poked through the house. Dak was hidden under a pile of sheets and blankets, tucked away between cushions in the corner of the room where we all slept. The soldiers did not go into that room.

My mother was in the kitchen. My father stood in the hallway. Suddenly, two soldiers pinned him to the wall. One soldier went into the kitchen. He hit my mother with the back of his hand across her cheek. My father strained against the khaki arms holding him back. Aïcha screamed and buried her face in the back of my mother's skirts. I just stood there. They did not hit my father, not my sister, not me, only Mama. The room was red before my eyes. Then they left. Dak hadn't made a sound.

When the soldiers had gone, my father wiped the blood from my mother's mouth. Her eyes were wide. He kept shaking his head slowly. I couldn't speak. The only sound was Aïcha sobbing dully into my mother's knees.

I found Dak. She was motionless underneath the sheeting bales. When I stroked her, she twitched an ear and opened her eyes. Something in them said she understood.

Our house stayed silent. I think it was my mother who first spoke.

'They weren't older than early twenties,' she said to no-one in particular, then looked at me. 'They were scared, Samir.'

I nodded.

'Scared of the NLF,' my father said. He thumped his fist in his palm. 'Scared, just like us.'

My parents explained that we'd been caught between the National Liberation Front and the French; in the middle somehow. I nodded. We didn't speak about the incident again. On the day we got independence, Dak barked. I think she understood.

When I was twenty-five, I moved to France. I never married. Never owned another dog.

Blind Date

Fiona loved French food. When a teaching job in Lyons was offered, she couldn't resist. It was not long before she needed a diet, but it had to be one with which she could live. So she noted down all she ate and soon had notes to fill a book. She tempted a publisher, no lean feat in the day of diet miracles. But she had a hook: snails.

Snails as protein. She collected them in a wicker basket after early morning rains lushed the banks of the Rhone. The local chefs were only too happy to lift their lids to the engaging young woman from England who would point at their pots and indicate that she would like a look inside. They showed her how to clean the snails, to sieve them three times, four times, five, to scrape the muddy froth from the top of the boiling pots. Not once did she hear scalded squeals.

But it was not enough to swap the heavy garlic butter sauce for parsley chopped in garlic broth. She needed to know much more about the creatures that would launch her book. So one day, from the university where she worked in the Tourism Department, she posted a request for information on snails and in an Internet group on molluscs.

The only live molluscs Fiona had ever seen were brown bearded barnacles on an English seaside pier. The Tourism Department of the university had sold the hard-boiled Lyons entrepreneurs the prospect of a new market: handicapped tourists. Fiona worked with deaf-mute students.

Her students knew the trade, but had yet to master English and computers. They would gather in her campus office and she would show them how she used her tools: 'You can use the Internet for networking and private correspondence,' Fiona wrote on a flip chart. 'You may even find like-minded electronic pals.'

She would take her students to the local cafés and coach them in toning down their sometimes exaggerated gestures, train them to read English lips of different accents and give them clues: 'Body language is different in the business world. Read it well, but take it with a grain of salt. Trust your intuition.'

Her students saw she was one of them, not just in her love of the city and its food, but in the way she explored new possibilities with them. 'The Internet is great for research. You can find anything out there if you just look. I even found material on *mollusca*.'

They smiled. An English woman who loved snails. When they ate out together, Fiona always ordered snails.

And it was the snails that introduced her to Yves. When she posted her "snails" request, it was Yves who directed her to *mollusca*. A computer analyst in Nice, he loved all things English, especially the language free of the diacritics that sprung from his native tongue like tiny blades to twist a life of school dictations failed.

His hobby, though, was snails: studying and eating them. 'Snails belong to the mollusc family,' he wrote. 'Snails in France are just common land snails of the Helix species. But there's a magnificent specimen in the London Museum.' He told her about their habitat, their nutrient value, their habits: 'Snails have teeth, thousands of them.'

Nibble, munch....

She told him about her diet, about the book. She told him how the snails had been the hook.

Yves wanted to practise his English and it was not long before their conversations went beyond snails to become a weekday Net chat of "getting to know you." Fiona told him where she worked, told him what she did. She did not tell him that he would never hear her voice other than through the tone of written electronic words. She did not tell him she could neither speak nor hear.

'I'm six foot tall and thin, ' he wrote. 'My hair's all there and it's dark brown, like my eyes. I enjoy my food, particularly snails.' The words grinned out green at her.

Fiona giggled and straightened her glasses. 'I'm five foot six and slim now, but I like my food, particularly French.' She added a :) 'How could I not, living in Lyons?' She brushed her hair back from her face. It was the sort of hair halfway between a crinkle and a curl, a barley-sugar blonde that frothed about her shoulders at the slightest hint of damp in the air. 'I have blonde curly hair,' she wrote. 'My eyes are blue, or grey sometimes.'

Weekends brought a pause to their chats. A modem at home was beyond Fiona's budget since her studio of rustic chic in the Old Town of Lyons was greedy for her salary. I'll get one when the book's published, she thought, popping a piece of Brie in her mouth. Nibble, munch.... She leant back on the self-upholstered sofa, a glass of table red in her hand and picked at the cheese.

Her mind ran through Yves' Friday message. 'Bon weekend,' he'd wished. He had little respect for the latest law demanding purity for his mother tongue.

He would sometimes delight her with whole sentences in French made up of mostly English words.

Monday mornings always brought a note from him to start the week. Sometimes it was late and then she would feel a little tug in her chest at the empty shell. The Net on detour, you never really knew...then a little trip in her throat would tell her the highway was open again as the words MESSAGE WAITING lit up.

She told him when her diet book proposal flew. He wrote back in support. When it landed and was retained, he was the first she told.

'A month to finish,' she wrote. 'I'll have to work flat out. Forgive me if I speak of nothing else.' Nibble, munch. She bit a leftover breakfast croissant. 'It's going to be published. The pressure's off. The snails did it.' Her fingers tripped over the keys. Nibble, munch.... She bit a bite of Brie and baguette.

'The book's out!' She hit the exclamation mark. 'Nibble, munch,' she mouthed.

She told him about Sarah, her childhood friend who worked for the publisher handling her book.

'Fiona, they want you to do a signing at Waterstone's,' Sarah's fax rolled its tongue out on her desk at home. 'A Friday and a Saturday morning. It'll be over by noon. You have to. It's promotional. I'll be there. Don't worry. It'll be OK. Love, Sarah.'

Fiona knew Sarah would calm and shield her at the signing. Fiona preached to her students with the calm of a lagoon, but in practice her gestures flooded her face and shoulders like waves rippling, then almost crashing with mounting emotion.

Nibble, munch.... I'll have to stop nibbling, Fiona thought. She knew she had broken all the rules. She'd let herself go. The waiting time between submission of the final manuscript and publication had taken a load off her and she had succumbed to between-meal tidbits. She'd been taken in by the elongated shadow the sun cast in the afternoon, ignoring the truth of the rounder one it cast at midday.

And now they wanted her to come to London and sign copies. She'd have to get those pounds off quickly. They were bound to show. No more bread and Brie. No more croissant, no more éclair. She had to be the proof of her own method. No more nibble munch.

'I have to go to London,' she emailed Yves. 'To sign the book.'

'I'll be there for work,' Yves replied. 'Maybe we could meet?'

'But I'll be busy Friday and Saturday morning.'

'I could wait in the London Museum—the Helix, you know.'

'But I wouldn't be finished before the evening.'

'Meet you in Soho, the Groucho Club.'

SERVER ERROR the letters blinked. The Net was down. Too much traffic. No, they didn't know when it would be up and running again.

Fiona reached for the last remains of carbs and fats, but stopped midway to her mouth. I'll just not turn up at the Groucho, she thought.

Fiona arrived in London on Friday morning. Sarah was at the airport and stayed by her side all through the signing at Waterstone's. Sarah did the talking and patrons quietly offered their purchases for Fiona's signature.

'Sarah, I can't go to the Groucho. He doesn't know. I'd rather take the next flight home.' She remembered other blind dates when the guy lost his tongue and stammered off on his way. And for those that weren't blind, the hours stretched past initial shyness into elastic bands of incomprehension, exhausting her nerves more than her muscles. If only she'd told him. It could have worked. He seemed kind enough. He had wanted to meet her.

Sarah left Fiona at the airport and dropped off the remains of the promotional material back at her office. It was late, around 10:30. She was relieved to see the entrance light of the publisher's and pretended to ignore the lanky figure on the steps. As she took her keys from her beige leather tote, the man pulled his hand from his pocket without a word. Sarah froze. He held out a small white card. She took it in with a glance. And then a smile melted her face.

Sarah ushered Yves to her office as he explained how he'd waited at the Groucho all evening, how Fiona hadn't turned up, how he was so worried. Sarah took a sheet of creamy paper from the pad on her period desk and scribbled wet inky words that she carefully blotted.

On Sunday afternoon the doorbell lamp flashed a ring. Fiona opened the door. A tall thin youngish man with brown hair and brown eyes stood on the porch. She knew it was Yves. Her heart thumped. Her eyes raced over his faded jeans, the white T-shirt, the cropped brown leather jacket, the horn-rimmed glasses…he'd never mentioned the glasses. Her mind flashed in cadence with her eyes as her fingers fiddled with the folds of her skirt.

Yves held out a box with a transparent top. Tilting her head to one side, Fiona smiled and accepted the chocolate molluscs as his fingers flurried perfect signs: 'We do have a common language, after all,' they said, their accent distinctly French.

Eyes to See

I'm on the Swiss Intercity from Zürich to Geneva and have just left my husband back in Vienna. I just walked away. And I cried, as I know he will when he finds my note on the dining room table: 'We don't see things with the same eyes.'

I slept surprisingly well on the night train, but this is the day route and grey hills roll down from the mountains. We will soon be in Berne and then only a couple of hours to Geneva where I must start all over again.

Green swirls from the landscape against the grey of the sky and my eyes slowly close.

'Stop! Sit here,' a woman's voice says.

I open my eyes. We have just left Berne. Bright red, black and gold bustle in the doorway as a woman steers a young boy before her, one arm outstretched, the other dragging a suitcase. She stops in the seat in front of mine. The boy must have taken a seat by the window. From her manner, as she peels off her cropped red leather jacket, it must be one facing the wrong way. I have always hated travelling with my back to my destination.

The child does not make a sound. The woman pulls off her soft black hat and black hair springs from the grasp of now loosened hairpins. Her fingers tuck back the stray hairs as she turns about and scans the compartment. Her underwear glows through her white nylon blouse with its frilled collar and cuffs. She sits down.

I feel exhausted. Smoke rises from the seat in front of me—first in almost perfect rings, then in slow jets, the sort that might come from the nostrils of an ageing dragon. My eyes close again.

'Watch it! You're going to sit on my son,' the woman's voice shrieks.

I open my eyes. We are leaving Lausanne. A man in his late forties, early fifties, large in a soft sort of way, towers in the space in front of my seat. He reminds me of my husband.

'I'm sorry,' the man says.

'You should watch what you're doing. My boy has problems with his eyes.'

'Sorry,' the man says again and sits down on the seat across the aisle, directly in my line of vision. He looks back to the seat he just tried to sit in, then over at the woman, across at the boy.

'Why are you staring at me like that?' the woman says.

'Pardon?'

'Why are you staring?'

There is a pause.

'Hush, dear.' (This to her son.) 'Maman is here.' And then to the man again: 'Well, what's wrong with you?'

The man smiles and his eyes look towards me. 'I am blind,' he says.

'Completely?'

'Yes,' he says and laughs.

'But you were looking at me. Where is your cane?'

The man raises his hand and a cane telescopes from his sleeve.

'That's splendid,' the woman says. 'Then there is hope for my son.'

'Didn't you notice?'

'No,' she says. 'I thought you were trying to pick me up.'

He laughs.

'I thought you were trying to pick me up.'

'I was,' said my husband. 'And I did, didn't I?'

We laughed about our first meeting when he'd tripped and fallen into my arms in the café in Vienna where I used to breakfast. The account of the incident became an ice breaker at dinner parties during the first years of our twenty-year marriage. Then, I was well-loved, alive and living in Vienna.

'What's your name?' the woman asks.

'Beau.'

'Well, then. Hi! I'm Belle.'

The man's eyes droop, but he laughs again, and strokes a palm over his thinning scalp. He isn't handsome, but there is something warm, trustworthy about him. Just like my husband, way back. Way back when.

I don't know when things changed, when I stopped trusting my husband, when he stopped trusting me. It's a little like what they say about pregnant women, or about people in love. When that state is yours then you see it in others. But there are times when you don't want to see. I'm no longer sure which of us cheated first, or if in fact we cheated at all. Neglect is something that just creeps in and only later cries out for justification.

The ticket collector comes into the compartment and the man holds out his pass.

'He is blind,' the woman says. 'But he sees everything.' The blind man smiles.

The woman leans forward and says in a loud whisper: 'Are you sure you can't see?'

'No. I can't see.'

'Why are you looking at me like that if you can't see?' She sits back.

'Your voice,' he says.

'My son, Billy, goes to school in Berne. I do this trip weekly: Berne-Geneva-Berne.'

The boy's arm reaches across and holds out a toy donkey. The man squeezes it and it makes a noise. Eee Aaa.

'Do you work?' the woman says.

'I'm a clerk. I stamp papers.'

'How do you know what to stamp?'

'I can feel. I've been doing it for years. It's all based on trust. In yourself. In others.'

She laughs. 'And there I was thinking you wanted to pick me up.'

The man takes out a cigarette, feels it to his lips and the woman lights it with a red lighter.

Then she lights her own cigarette. They both smoke.

'Can I have your phone number?' she says. The man fumbles in the pocket of his jacket and gives her a card. 'At work,' he says.

'You are so well-dressed,' the woman says. 'Your life. It gives me hope for my son.' She says to the boy: 'Go and sit with the man.'

The boy does not move. I hear shuffling. 'He won't,' she says. 'His mother is everything.' She laughs and draws on her cigarette. 'Can I give you my phone number?'

'Please write it down,' he says.

She scribbles and hands him an orange slip of paper. The man puts it in his pocket.

'Are you married?' she says.

The man shakes his head. 'But I have help. The essential things.'

'And your work? You are very clean. Do you dress yourself?'

'I follow the advice I am given. It's easier with someone there. Mornings are fine. If I feel there's a spot or if someone notices and tells me, and, if I have time, I change.'

She sighs. 'You are so clean.' Then she stubs out her cigarette. 'My son cannot dress himself.'

'That's because he is always supervised.'

'Yes. He is at school all week. He comes home weekends. I go to fetch him.

Like today.' She stops and says: 'The children don't always understand. Billy is happy, but doesn't notice when the children tease him.'

Then there is a pause in their conversation. I lean back and think about what they have said. I think about the way they talked, too. Direct. Innocent. Saying what they thought.

My husband and I talked like that once. Then we began to talk in riddles, assuming the years had allowed us to read each other's minds. Perhaps neither of us had really read what had been there.

Then, as if out of nowhere, I again hear the woman's voice: 'Billy says how wonderful life is. Every morning he says that. Don't you Billy?'

There is no answer.

'Do you have to pay on the train?'

'When I'm alone,' the man says. 'When someone is with me, they don't pay.'

'Same here. I travel free,' she says. 'But not on the plane.'

Billy is fidgeting. I cannot see.

'Stop that,' she says. 'Billy, stop it!' Then she is calm. 'He likes music, you know.'

'Does he play?' the man asks.

'The piano? No. He sings. Sing Billy.'

'No,' says the boy.

The man looks at me. I wonder if he sees me watching.

'What do you see?' the woman says. 'Do you see black? What did you see at the beginning? Now?'

'Nothing,' says the man. 'It's been too long ago. People only see black when they remember. I have nothing to remember, so I see nothing.' I wonder what nothing looks like.

The train pulls in to Geneva's main station. The man unfolds his white cane and gets his bag down from the rack. Then he makes his way to the door and steps down. He says nothing. Does not wave.

'Goodbye,' says the woman. The man doesn't answer.

One more stop to go until the airport. I settle back and think of my husband finding my note. 'Billy, what do you see?' the woman suddenly says to the boy.

'People.'

'What?'

'People.'

'How many?'

'Lots,' the boy says and then starts to sing.

The train pulls into the station. The woman puts on her red leather jacket and tugs the brim of her hat deep over her eyes. As we reach for our bags up on the rack our hands touch. The woman turns her head. 'My son is blind,' she says. 'He cannot help me.'

I hoist my bag down and, stopping to catch my breath, I watch the woman urge her son from the train. I step down to the platform and my vision blurs.

Closer Than Comfort

Holly lay on her back on the sofa, her head in her mother's lap, and pretended she was lying in a bed of sand. Sand always steadied undesired movements. She held up a black and white snapshot she had just found tucked away in a biscuit tin under the window seat.

Maybe she's like me, Holly thought. Maybe Mother also has her own world. Maybe she also stores her memories as images; the only difference is that hers are on paper.

Holly's hands twitched, making the photo flutter.

'Your father had a way with women,' Holly's mother said. 'You're old enough now. I can mention these things.'

Holly took the photo with both hands and fingered it. He was good-looking, in a Fred Astaire sort of way. The dark hair slicked back with a part on the side, the double-breasted jacket buttoned over wide loose trousers. Why, she almost expected him to tap-dance off into the room, just as she'd seen Fred Astaire do with Leslie Caron in *Daddy Longlegs*. Holly was fifteen and only had a vague recollection of the man her mother said disappeared from their lives. Disappeared. Just like that.

'He told one of his lovers...that her breasts were small,' Holly's mother said as she stroked her daughter's curly red hair.

Holly jerked her head. Her mother stopped stroking. Why does she have to fiddle with my hair like that, Holly thought and stretched out her arms, as if the further she held her father away from her, the better she would be able to see him, and the easier it would be to understand her mother.

'So what did she do?' Holly's mother said, oblivious of her daughter's attempt at control. 'The silly goose went and had plastic surgery. Do you know what he said when she asked him if he liked her that way?'

Holly shook her head. She squinted at the man in the photo, tried to focus on what his answer could be. Then her hands trembled, and stopped.

'He said he liked her the way she was before. He'd just said that her breasts were small.' Holly's mother's voice was low. Then it brightened. Holly caught the tremor. She sensed how her mother pulled herself together and knew she wouldn't crash into tears, the way Holly was apt to do.

Holly turned her head, stole a look at her mother's face and then nestled gingerly into the ample bosom.

'He always went after married women. That way he could stay free, you know.'

Holly stiffened as her mother began stroking her hair again.

'He'd ignore women at first, and when they'd start worrying that they weren't attractive enough, when they started doubting...that's when he'd pounce.' Holly's mother paused. 'He once told me to dye my hair red, you know.'

Holly didn't answer. She felt a heat rush up her neck. Her mother could make her so angry at times.

'So I did.' Holly's mother said and shifted. 'It took ages to grow out.' Holly wriggled in her mother's lap. 'He'd never have needed to ask you to do that,' Holly's mother added.

Holly sat up stiffly and placed the photo on top of the biscuit tin. Then she began rocking.

Holly rocked often, particularly at school. 'Pay attention,' snapped Mrs Ayckborn, her English teacher. Holly tried, but nothing kept her interest for long, not the words, not the other pupils. She was happiest just drawing pictures of birds, like the rosellas she saw fly from the trees outside her window. And she also loved playing chess. At lunchtime she would take her sandwiches and go to the common room while most of the other pupils ran around outside. She would sit in the corner where two benches met and set out a board with chess pieces, the small plastic ones that sat securely in their holes. Then, drawing her knees up to her chest, she stretched out an arm and played with an imaginary partner, always the same one, one without a name. She just knew that her partner was not a girl nor a woman.

'You're clever, Holly,' her maths teacher said to her a few weeks before her final exams. Mr Fulton would coach her at lunchtime on Thursdays. 'You've got everything in boxes in your head. You just have to find a way to open them.'

Holly saw a box and watched its lid open. Birds in magenta and green flew out, their wings flapping. A smaller grey bird tried to fly in their tailwind. Buffeted, stunned, it fell back into the box. Holly shivered.

Holly sat her exams and managed to scrape through. When she refused to go out and took to staying in her room for days on end, her mother rang the local doctor.

'She won't go out,' her mother said on the phone. 'Unless the weather is fine. Then she goes to the same spot down the road where the bush starts and sits under the tall eucalyptus. She always comes back after a while, but then she just watches old films on her video. No, she doesn't seem depressed. Now that school's over she even seems happy. She could go out with others her age. She's such a pretty girl now, but she doesn't seem to be aware of that, nor even care. She seems to live out of reality. She says she wants a computer. That will just make things worse. Imagine, alone with a computer all day.'

Holly was eighteen when she was diagnosed as suffering from Asperger syndrome. 'It's a mild form of autism,' the specialist said. 'She has a good memory, vivid visualisation, imagination and strong powers of concentration. She should be able to find work.'

Holly was present when the doctor gave his views to her mother, but she heard them as if through a third person, as if she were watching herself through the eyes of the doctor and those of her mother. She saw a young woman she didn't quite recognise: tall, slim, dressed in grey wool, curly red hair twisting past her shoulders.

'Socially,' the doctor said, 'life will be difficult, but she can try.'

'She always tries, Doctor,' her mother said. 'I don't always see it like that though, I must admit. She can get so angry.'

'She needs structure,' the doctor said. 'The first time she does something new is always the hardest for her. But she has logic. She will find her own way.'

When Holly and her mother arrived back home, Holly screamed: 'You're suffocating me. I don't care if I'm different. I'm not like you.' She stormed to her room, slammed the door.

In her room Holly sat down on the floor in a corner. She twirled her fingers through her hair that tousled over one shoulder and turned on her radio on the floor beside her. She turned it on low.

'I'm leaving town,' a woman's voice said. 'Gotta sell all. Books. Toshiba laptop.'

Holly heard the brand name. She knew what it stood for since she had a subscription to a computer magazine and devoured every article. She wasn't always taken in by the ads, but she knew the brand had real keys, the sort you could pound all day and never get tired. Or so they said. You could use it anywhere. Journalists did, she had read. She imagined a woman in khaki clothes sitting way high in the hills, in Afghanistan, knees up, rushing out a report on the conflict below. Holly knew she could get images on the laptop. She'd never dared try one out in the shop: that would have meant starting a conversation with someone she didn't know.

Then the woman on the radio gave her phone number. Holly didn't need to jot it down—she remembered it, saying it after the first digit as if all along she had known it by heart. But talk on the phone? No, she couldn't do that.

The laptop. The laptop. Holly took a deep breath. Here goes, she thought, and dialled the number. The woman's name was Moira.

Moira described the way to her place at North Sydney as if reading from a detailed map. Holly closed her eyes and tried to visualise the route. The next day she took her own map of the city and traced her way across town, following the winding streets as if knowing she would find her way out of the maze. Holly loved maps for she was scared of new turns, new turns in the road and new turns in her life. The laptop, the laptop.

Moira was a tall, large woman dressed in a dark red caftan. 'It's small,' Moira said as she ushered Holly into her flat. 'Self-contained. No room for junk.'

Holly looked about the bed-sitter. It was not unlike her own room: a cupboard, a bed, a desk, a TV. A desktop computer was on the desk, and on the floor, lid open, sat the laptop. Holly looked up to the white ceiling and then to the cupboard. A red and blue parrot gazed down upon her.

'It's not real,' Moira said, following Holly's gaze. 'But it's fun.'

'The laptop?' said Holly.

'That's fun, too,' Moira said with a smile. 'I'll make you a good price and I'll throw in the parrot. Would you like the parrot?'

Holly shook her head. 'I just want the laptop.'

Four years later Holly got a job as a programmer in the Northern Business District. She'd applied on-line and done a test. She was good at spotting faults in code patterns. She moved away from her mother and rented a furnished flat down by the Harbour Bridge not far from where she'd bought the laptop. Holly's company let her work from home and gave her a high-speed computer. Holly put her old laptop away. She had always wanted more memory and a high-speed connection. Funny, she thought. When you have something you always want more, and she was getting it now. Maybe, she wasn't so different from other people after all.

Holly dropped into a chat group on the Net and lurked for a while. It's easy to post a message, step back, then watch from a safe distance, she thought. She asked if anyone knew how to fix a flaw in her software. Two days later she had a reply.

Holly was nervous when she saw the message addressed to her, but knowing she had time to analyse what it said calmed her down.

His name was Sean and he lived across the world. Scotland. He advised her. They wrote. He was also a programmer. And he was there, out there. Holly and Sean corresponded off and on for six months. He became...a soul mate of sorts, Holly liked to think...and at a safe distance. Everyone said you had to be careful of people you didn't know. Holly was careful of anything she didn't know. But once again she had visions of wings, only this time they were those of an angel, an angel in a red kilt—it was the only image she could relate to.

'Don't you think we should meet?' Sean wrote one day.

Holly had always refused to let herself be cornered. 'My friends say I'm mad to have friends I can't see,' she wrote back. 'But, I need to see.' Holly didn't tell Sean she hardly had friends, that she preferred to be alone in her own special world, a world of which he had now become a part.

'I agree with them,' was Sean's reply. 'Are you scared I won't like you?'

Holly found herself shrugging her shoulders. 'You like me already. I can feel it.' Holly read back the words. I can feel it? Feel it? Holly's mind raced. It was a bit like playing chess. It was like the thrill of placing the pieces, knowing she might win, might not lose. It was logical, in a way.

'How can you feel it?' Sean wrote.

'It's on another plane.' Holly's heart began to beat faster. 'It's got nothing to do with body language,' Holly wrote. 'I think I can see you.'

'So shall I come?' Sean wrote. 'I'll send you a photo.'

Holly giggled. Then she started to hiccup. Her chest began to ache as her face became hot and her hands became clammy. She wondered what he would say if he knew she wasn't, wasn't quite like other people.

Two weeks later a note from Sean arrived: 'I'm coming next week. Please be at the airport.' Clipped to the note was a black and white passport-type photo. Holly turned it over. The words "Love Sean" were written in red on the back. He's forgotten the comma, Holly thought.

Holly slept little the night before Sean's plane was due to arrive. Her mind went over the facts as she thought she knew them: he was a year older than she was; he came from about as far away as one could; his hair was black; he had travelled all over. But she needed Sean's image and so took out his photo. She traced a finger down the side of his face, along the jaw line and over the dimple in his chin. There she hesitated before tracing back up to the top of his dark-haired head.

Holly thought how she'd never dared mention exchanging photos. She didn't really want a photo of Sean, even now. She was sure she would have known him when he arrived. Yet she needed to see even though his words had already built a programme in her mind. Not having a photo would have made it easier to run away, she thought. She could still run away, not accept a second date—or even a first one.... How could someone come all the way to Australia just for a date? She was sure she couldn't handle it.

At the airport a lanky young man with dark hair came towards her. Holly froze.

'You told me you had red curly hair, but you never said it was the colour of autumn,' he said. Then he cupped her face in his hands, held her a moment and then kissed her tenderly on her right cheek. Holly felt dizzy. She suddenly thought of her father. She saw him drawing her to him and placing a kiss on her forehead. The picture flooded her mind and pieces began to fall into place.

'This is so strange,' Holly said. I feel I know you, she thought.

Holly didn't know what she wanted to expect. She had found a growing closeness to Sean through their messages, but it had seemed more an affinity of minds, like what one might feel for a favourite teacher, even a father, a feeling that maybe someone understood. With others it had only ever gone one way. An on-off thing. Bit. Bit. Like what she had had with her mother.

But this was interactive and Holly was reacting. Holly spooled her mind back to the things Sean had mentioned: how he didn't like groups, how he'd never known his father, how he loved to dance, how he'd said that he wanted to see rosellas fly in the sun. Holly grappled for structure, for a familiar framework.

Then she slipped her arms around Sean's body, closed her eyes and hung on tight.

Mimosa

J en sat at a table in the hospital reception and gazed out of the window. The afternoon sun was locked in a smoke haze, charred wattle trees stood like stick men. Tears pricked her eyes. She wiped a hand over her cheek, saw grime on her palm and rubbed it clean on her jeans. Two fists of paper were already on the floor as she again took up her pen.

Dear Monsieur Montalbon, she wrote. She crumpled up the paper and began once more.

Dear Pierre,... She stared at the name and then scratched through the words. How was she going to tell this man on the other side of the world about a woman he had loved a lifetime ago?

> Dear Mr Montalbon,
> We've never met, but I'm sure the name "Springwood" means something to you. You may have seen the candles and the tiny—how to describe them?—gourd-like receptacles my mother marketed under that name. She advertised her products in pamphlets and on the Internet...

This was too much. Pictures and words couldn't hope to show what went into her mother's work.

She'd made the gourds from Eucalyptus, from silver-top stringy bark. Springwood was full of it, and full of wattle.

> She made essences from wattle and eucalypts. The fragrances fuelled her dreams.

Jen scratched out 'dreams' and then the whole sentence.

> My mother only ever worked with what was already there.

Jen propped her head on her hand. I'll just write it as it was, she thought. I can always go back and cross out the things I can't tell him.

> The dark brown receptacles she carved resembled the bud cups of the stringy bark gum, and she smeared them with translucent pastes that were, in fact, the trapped scents of eucalyptus and wattle.

Jen's eyes were now wet but she kept on scribbling across the page.

I'm telling you all this so that you understand what really happened. It's about my mother, it's about Lucia. And in a way, you are next of kin.

Jen sat back in her chair, her hair fell back from her face. She had to go on.

You may know wattle as acacia. Your acacia—my mother told me that you call it "mimosa"—seems to be of a singular kind. Despite its fragrant smell—so unlike our wattle—the moment you place your mimosa in a vase, it begins to droop. Not even a Lalique vase, she said, can keep it alive.

Jen wiped her eyes with her left hand. I have to get a grip on myself, she thought, then sniffed deeply and continued to write.

The town of Springwood clusters around a Blue Mountains highway and is split by the rail line from Sydney to Katoomba.
This was where we lived. Our house was just one mile from the highway, out by a ridge by Clarinda Falls. It was made of sandstone; the veranda posts were made of ironbark, a timber hard as its name, and so were the doors and the shutters, which were painted a rich bottle green. These shutters might remind you of the South of France, which would be deceptive. The shutters in France do not do the same thing as ours in Australia. Our house had a veranda to keep out the heat; the shutters kept out the cold snaps of our mountain winters.

I grew up there alone with my mother, surrounded by the scents of the bush: the tang of gum leaves, the rich aroma of rain-showered soil. The smell of smoke would at times cut through those scents when gusts whipped the trees and the heart-shaped leaves of the mountain gum became brittle in the hot wind.

This year it's been hot and very dry. Strong winds raged through the bush. And I volunteered for the fire brigade.

Again Jen sat back and gazed out of the window. She stared at the bushland and, as if in a trance, watched the past days spool through her mind.
Fires forged through the gullies, the high winds doubling their spread and the oils of the gum trees vaporized so quickly that even the air exploded. Waxy leaves crackled and spat as the flames raced through the mountain treetops. Back burning was difficult in those conditions. With my helpers, two gangly boys, we trained the muzzles of our drip torches onto the brush, but the winds were strong and kept changing direction, forcing the flames back upon us. All we could do was aim the hoses from our tanker truck onto the ground at our feet and just beyond, keeping it moist until the wind died.
I'd just dropped the boys off at their homes behind the station. Those grey fibro houses would have been tinder had they been on the outskirts of town.

The tanker had to be refilled with water for the next shift and I had to wrestle the gears of the truck to get it back to base. I'd just got into my old Corolla and was in the centre of Springwood by the corner pub facing the station when the radio call came about the fire on the ridge over Sassafras, just three miles away. I clenched the steering wheel. The fires were close to our house.

I phoned through to the central and tore off past the pedestrians clumped at the corner. I went up through the gears, peak revs in each one, until I was doing seventy miles an hour down a patched and pitted bitumen road. The car rattled and shook as it clanked over the potholes and the muffler kept hitting its underside. Swerving to avoid one of the potholes, I put the outside wheels onto the road's soft edges. I swerved, lost control, then regained it. All I could see when I glanced at the rear-view mirror was stirred-up dust.

Then I saw thick smoke coming from the ridge over the gully. Mum used to take me for picnics to Sassafras Gully and she taught me to swim down past Clarinda Falls. Water. If only there was more of it now.

But the wind brought no rain; it just bent the boughs of the bordering gums and I had to keep my eyes fixed on the road. I had to get home. A bend was ahead. I knew the road backwards, and was going as fast as I could. But every bump on the muffler made me slow down for fear that I'd lose it, not really knowing if that was serious or not. I had to hang on for just one more bend.

Suddenly, to my left, a chain of exploding flames crashed through the treetops. The smoke was getting thicker and I could smell tar, and burning rubber. Then I saw the house. A sheet of flames veiled the one-storey structure that shimmered ghost-like through the hot orange red. Black smoke billowed in ugly thick coils from the rubber tyre that ringed the bed of a transplanted Waratah. The wildflower bush was ashen white; the once red tough petals now petrified.

I slammed on the brakes and got out of the car, pulling my cotton scarf over my nose and mouth. My eyes were smarting and I had to squint in order to see. I began coughing. It wasn't just the smoke; my heart thumped in my lungs.

The shutter doors were black with strips of glowing orange where the wind fanned them. The old sofa on the veranda was smouldering and blotches of black blistered flickering edges into the upholstery. I was standing just metres away when the veranda roof crashed under the weight of a falling stringy bark gum. The roof was made from shingles and tar and now the supporting beams were collapsing onto themselves. The tree and the wind-whipped embers had done their work as burning slats crashed over the three-step stairway to what was once grass.

Then I saw the body.

A certain terror of things moving beyond control must have blocked my perception. But it was a human body: white, singed and inanimate. I put my head down and ran at it. The smoke singed my eyes. Through the haze, I gasped for air. It was Mum. She was lying face down, that wonderful red hair singed to the scalp. Her legs were charred white and the muslin at her shoulders was like ragged black lace where the skin had been burned. Her arms were coated in what looked like soot, except for the parts that exposed livid flesh.

She must have been trying to run. Must have tripped on that long skirt of hers. It had been the blue of a clear sky but now its crisp pleats were blackening in a dying glow. I beat at the fabric and it crumbled away. Coughing, I touched her throat. Then I grabbed my mobile from my belt and called through to Emergency.

'I'm out past the rifle club, end Bee Farm Road. Got a third degree here. Still got a pulse.' I tried to scream it was Mum, but the words stuck in that place between concept and sound as the answer crackled back: 'You'll have to get to Katoomba. The ambulances are out. Springwood Hospital's cut off.'

I touched the soft white skin of my mother's legs, but it didn't blanch. She didn't seem to feel pain and I thought that maybe her nerve endings were destroyed. 'I'll give it a go.'

'Good luck, love.'

I rolled Mum onto her back and then picked her up. She was birdlike in my arms. I just stood there a moment. Her head lolled, she was slipping away. I eased her onto the back seat of the car, but her head bumped against the far door. Sorry. Sorry? Yes, sorry. So sorry.

I slammed the door, threw in reverse gear and spun back towards the road. The stringy bark boughs along the embankment were drooping, their leaves singed. The wind had died down, but there was still a fog of smoke, so heavy even the sun couldn't pierce it. I raced back past the cemetery and the fire station. The tankers were all out. I veered onto the highway towards Katoomba.

Cars with orange headlights were fleeing towards Sydney. Katoomba was the other way, but I feared I'd never make it. I jammed my foot on the accelerator, ignoring the banging muffler. Suddenly it clanked one last time, but I raced on as if driven by the engine's loud throaty roar.

In Katoomba they took my mother away. Come back later, they said. She'll need a few days.

I got back into my car and backtracked to the house, slowly, the engine rasping. As I drew up two fire fighters were training their hoses onto what was left. The sandstone walls rose from a sloppy debris of everything we had: Mum's work, our life, my own hopes and dreams, all reduced to a smouldering rubble. I just stood there.

There was a public shelter in Katoomba they'd converted from a school gym and I spent the next few nights there. Families huddled in the corners. Empty mattresses lined the walls. The wooden floor gleamed with fresh polish and the sweet acrid odour made me want to retch. But I couldn't. I breathed in deeply and coughed as the smell of ammonia burned the insides of my nostrils. Bottles of water were passed around, but I couldn't get rid of the taste of smoke.

All night there was coughing. Here and there kids were crying. I opened my eyes. A woman in the corner was rocking to and fro, but what I saw was Mum, prostrate on the ground.

The next day I was out again with the brigade and I tried to block Mum from my mind. She loved you, you know. Would things have been different if you had been here?

I had the boys with me again and had to give them my full attention. But every blackened stump, every new coil of smoke brought the vision of Mum in front of the house. I needed to know how she was. I phoned the hospital, but they said it was still too early to know. Too soon to come. So I worked on with the boys and tried to keep my mind off anything but fighting those flames and saving what we could. It was three days before I saw Mum again.

She'd been moved to a small two-bed room with a window. The first bed was empty, like a buffer for hers. A translucent cuff covered her nose and was linked through a tube to a box with a dial and blinking red dots. Her head was bandaged and so were her arms, which splayed out over the sides of the bed. From her right wrist she hung on a drip. A sheet covered her loosely from her neck to the foot of the bed. The room was pale grey like the wisps of smoke in the sky outside. A watercolour calendar picture was on the wall—the bush as it used to be.

The doctor came in. Was I the daughter? he asked. Was there anyone else? I said yes and shook my head. Her burns were serious. He looked at the sheet and my eyes followed his. She'd need grafting, he said with a voice as flat as the covers of the empty bed he now leant on. I couldn't bear to think of what her sheet hid. Then his voice cut in again. The ground transport had taken too long, he said. There was a risk of renal infection and the prognosis was not good. She was delirious, he continued and moved closer to me. 'Delirium's a funny thing,' he said softly. 'All sorts of stuff starts spilling out. Then there's silence, and here and there, a flash of lucidity.'

All of a sudden Mum opened her eyes and stared straight at me. She opened her lips and as I knelt down beside her I smelled the wet odour of burning tyres. 'Pierre', she said and then closed her eyes. The next day she said my name, but then she said 'Pierre', and then I lost her.

When I came the following day they'd taken the cuff from her nose and the tube and machine were on the night table. I'd taken it as a sign that she was improving, that there was still hope. Her eyes rolled. It was as if she was waiting for something.

Then all of a sudden she thrashed with her legs and the movement dragged the sheet from her neck, exposing her shoulders and breast. The skin of her shoulders was red and dry, and large blotches of white ran from her clavicle over her chest. I gingerly pulled the sheet back to cover her. She did not flinch. But then her head crashed from left to right. Her eyes stared and those lashless eyelids flickered wildly then stopped. My pulse raced and just when I thought she had calmed, she jerked her arm with an unexpected movement that pulled at the drip and sent the stand crashing to the floor.

I grabbed for the bell, which was caught in the bedclothes. Pressed the button. Kept pressing. Now I knew what panic was. I was jamming the bell, wanting to rush out, but not daring to leave her alone, when a young nurse rushed in. The nurse righted the stand. Mum became still. The nurse grabbed the nasal cuff and fixed it over her face and set the ventilator in motion. Then she signed that I should leave.

Jen sat at the desk, her head in her hands. An eerie glow was tingeing the sky as if letting night fall at last. Her eyes were dry. 'Mum died last week,' she whispered. 'Two weeks since the fire at our house. I knew she wouldn't have wanted a funeral, so I asked if I could have her ashes. I didn't want to leave her with strangers. And you, you were so far away, and what were you now to her anyway?'

Jen felt her eyes moisten. 'They gave me a plastic grey box in a stiff white carry bag and I kept it next to my mattress in the corner of the gym.' Silent sobs now punctuated her words. 'I had to do something that would let me move on.' Jen took a deep breath and wiped her nose. 'Yesterday, in a bed at the end of our land, overlooking the gully, I planted seedpods of wattle and sprinkled them with her ashes.'

Jen took a fresh piece of paper.

> Dear Monsieur Montalbon,
> A woman you once loved passed away last week. Please accept my condolences.

A single drop of rain splatted against the glass, then another, and another until sheets of water were washing the window. Jen stared at the letter. Deliberately, eking the word out, she wrote Sincerely and added a comma. She paused, listening to the rain drumming against the pane, then folded the letter once, and once again, and slipped it into the back pocket of her jeans.

'Maybe tomorrow,' she whispered.

Western Rerun

Doris sat in the bus shelter clutching her walking stick. It was one of those sticks you could grasp in your hand. Doris lived in a home now. She had a bed-sitter, but she knew that help would be there should she need it. After Jack died, she'd sold the house and moved into the retirement home. Jack would never have given it up. It had been a gift from the government to thank returned soldiers for their war efforts up in New Guinea.

Jack didn't speak much about those efforts and when he did it was only to mention the good times. 'We'd never have made it without the fuzzy-wuzzy angels,' he'd say and then clamp down. 'Don't ask me about the Japs.' Doris never did.

Jack did well in his job at the hat factory and their life became comfortably suburban: the dunny out the back made way for a septic tank, a Holden stood in the carport. But something about Jack had changed. It wasn't a sudden thing. She only really noticed it now she had time to think back over the years. It sort of sneaked up on them. Jack was lucky; he retired before hats went out of fashion. But he seemed to lose interest in things about him, preferring to stay inside and watch Western reruns. He talked less and less. It seemed as if all he was interested in was the TV and the scones Doris made for Saturday tea. He loved the scones and the strawberry jam.

Doris sat in the bus and wondered at how things had changed. Shopping centres were everywhere. Even the post office where she'd pick up her pension was now in the middle of Westfield. She remembered the first time she'd gone by herself. She'd backed out and left when she saw the dusky sloe-eyed faces behind the counters. Asians. They were everywhere. She was used to it now. They were very polite, friendly. Just like us, she thought.

Doris made her way back to the bus stop. She was getting too tired to wander about. She sat down on the bench, patted her wool skirt over her knees and clutched her stick. Two schoolgirls in their blue uniforms, their blouses hanging out and their skirts hitched up their thighs whispered secrets. A middle-aged woman with shopping bags in each hand sat down by her side. Doris smiled. The woman ignored her.

Doris looked at her watch. Another ten minutes. A man, Asian, she thought, stood at the sign with the timetable. Maybe Japanese? He was very well dressed. What would Jack say to that. A dark mass, Doris thought, was trundling towards the bus stop. It was an Aboriginal woman. She'd never seen an Aboriginal this close. The woman fell. She was just a few yards away. The sound was awful. White muck spilled from her mouth and then she just lay there. No one moved. The schoolgirls stared. The woman by her side said: 'Drunken slob.'

Doris grabbed her stick, sat up and breathed deeply. Help her, she thought. Somebody help her. Then the Japanese man went over to the woman lying on the ground. He spoke into his mobile phone. Then he lifted the woman's head, and with his handkerchief wiped her face. Sirens screamed. They hoisted the woman onto a stretcher and rolled it into the ambulance. Doris' bus was approaching.

The Japanese man ran a finger down the timetable. Doris looked out of the bus window and her eyes met his. Suddenly, she felt very, very sad.

Bogeyman

Henry was Mum's friend first.

'You'll like Henry,' she said. 'He'll be staying the weekend.'

I nodded. I'd noticed Mum had been acting differently. We'd often sing songs together when we did the washing up. She'd taken to humming to herself. I liked it because her brown eyes would sparkle and she'd smile more. But somehow it was hard to sing along.

'What's that song?'

'Oh, nothing, dear.' Then she'd start up again to herself.

Henry was dark and lanky. He didn't push himself forward like some grownups did. He just smiled and said: 'Hi, Angie.'

I nodded and turned away to busy myself in the kitchen, my ears straining to hear every word.

'She's shy,' Mum said.

'So am I,' said Henry.

I think that was when I decided I liked Henry.

The next day Henry said, 'Want to take me for a walk in the bush?'

I nodded, took the hand he held out to me and led the way down the path.

The bush was dry and crackling, alive with noises. Twitching scales scuttled through the brush as kookaburras laughed across the treetops. It was as if the plants, even the rocks, were alive.

'That's where the bogeyman lives,' I whispered, pointing to a dark mouth half-hidden by banksia bushes. I tugged Henry's hand, drawing him closer. He made me feel safe, my hand in his large firm grip.

'Don't know if I can climb down there,' Henry said.

'Course you can. Look, there's a bit of path between the rocks. You can hold on to those bushes.'

The cave was perched on an outcrop of rock and brush on the other side of the creek—just above eye level.

I tugged again at Henry's hand. 'Come on. You can do it,' I said, running down to the creek. 'Go over the log.' I felt the flip of my ponytail between my shoulder blades as I landed on the other bank. Henry followed, wobbling a bit. But he only needed one step and he was over.

I clambered up the other side and waited just below the cave. 'Hurry up,' I urged under my breath. I watched him weave his long thin legs through the brush towards me.

'There's nothing here,' he said, his head just below the cave floor.

'Yes there is. It looks like a bed,' I hissed.

Henry hoisted himself to the edge of the opening. 'Just a couple of blankets. Let's go Angie,' he said.

'Wait for me!' I called, scrambling after him. I didn't want to be left alone there. I started to understand why Mum hummed.

I grabbed Henry's hand and grinned up at him. 'Want to hear a bell bird?'

'There aren't any round here.'

'Bet you. Listen to this,' and I pulled a light green stalk; I inspected it quickly, slipped it between my lips and sucked my breath in short bursts. A high metallic chirp shrilled back at us.

'Not bad,' Henry said. 'Guess you fooled them.'

'Sure did.' I smiled in triumph. We walked on until we came to a fork. 'Want to see the ghost house?' I ventured.

'Is it like the bogeyman's cave?' Henry raised both eyebrows.

'It's real. You can see it without going off the track.'

He gave in and we walked on hand in hand, swinging our arms in step. Then the track shrunk to single file. Banksia bushes and bottlebrush filled gaps between eucalyptus gums standing like sentries. The undergrowth thickened and we could go no further.

'Just a dead end,' Henry said. 'Come on, Angie. We have to get back.'

'Look! Over there through the bushes. That burnt-out house next to the gum with the blood running all down its trunk.'

'That's not blood, that's resin, and you know it.' He craned to see through the scrub.

'A man killed his wife and kids there,' I whispered.

Henry didn't say a word. He just squeezed my hand.

Henry came to stay the next weekend. And the next. And the next.

He'd let me snuggle into bed with him on a Sunday morning while Mum made breakfast. He'd tell me lovely horse stories. It was warm in his bed and I'd press myself against him. He smelled of hay. I could almost smell the horses, hear their gentle whinnies and feel their quivering flanks. It made me fizzle inside like bits of sherbet on my tongue.

Then all of a sudden he stopped coming. I wondered if the look in Mum's eyes had something to do with it. She stopped humming. She didn't even sing with me anymore. I missed him.

'What's wrong with Henry, Mum? Why doesn't he come anymore?'

'Henry? He went to America.'

'America?'

He'd left Mum. Just like Dad. Henry was just like the others.

With a little rub every day, my growing up erased him from my mind until there was almost nothing left. I finished high school and got a job as a typist. I spent less time at home. Mum and I got on all right; it was just that the song had gone from our house.

On my 19th birthday, Mum and I sipped a glass of sparkling wine.

'I want to go abroad, Mum,' I said.

She nodded.

I got a job in Geneva, typing at the UN. I never seemed to find time to write home. Just a card here and there. I'd go out with the girls from the typing pool, but whenever we'd meet up with men in the English pubs, I always found an excuse to leave before anyone wanted to bring me home.

One February morning, I looked out across the grey flat lake. Behind me droned the CNN news. I jolted as I heard the name of my home town.

'Flames moved in on Sydney's suburbs Friday, destroying houses as wind-fuelled bushfires raged across the hot and dry Southeast part of Australia,' clipped the voice of the newsreader.

I stared at the satellite pictures. My heart thumped as I glimpsed what must have been koala hides smouldering in wasteland parks, familiar houses scorched, some gutted. Panicking people were being herded onto buses bound for evacuation shelters. I switched off the set and picked up the phone.

'Don't worry, dear. The neighbours helped me hose the house down. You remember bushfires.'

'What about the bush down the back?'

'It's all still there.'

I started calling twice a day. I made my mother talk, talk about anything— as if endless words could shrink the distance.

'Remember Henry, Mum? What really happened to him?'

There was a short silence. 'He killed himself, dear. You must have been about eleven or so.'

'Why, Mum?'

'Well...one Sunday morning I came in to the guest room to say breakfast was ready and found you snuggled tight under the covers. I think I saw things in a different way that day. I thought you were both getting, well...you know... too close.'

'But, Mum...' I remembered how I had taken Henry's hand, had put it on the rise on my chest. But Henry had taken his hand away to hold my shoulder in a warm hug. I remembered being confused for a moment, but then it was gone.

'I suppose I thought something might happen to you. Thought I was losing you,…losing Henry.'

'Oh, Mum.'

'I told Henry to go, but couldn't bring myself to tell him why. He must have taken it quite badly, worse than I expected…He'd felt at home with us….' My mother's voice trailed off.

Rain fell on Tuesday. The fires no longer rated a place in the news as I made my last crisis call.

'It's over, dear,' my mother said. 'The bush is gone, but the house is safe.'

I took a deep breath and opened the window. A pale blue scrap of sky melted through the clouds over Geneva. Back in the bush, fresh shoots would soon sprout from charred eucalyptus branches.

Suddenly I knew I needed to see them grow again.

Flash Fiction in the Pure Slush Lifespan Series

from Work Lifespan Volume 5 – May 2022

I'll Scratch Yours

The day after her promotion, she received a phone call from one of the big wigs in her outfit. He ran a section – no, division; no, department – he was really big – on something Telco technical.

"I ring to congratulate you, Ms…"

"Candida."

"Yes, Ms Candida."

She was taken aback that someone so high up should ring her so soon. Later, would have been more understandable, not for the congratulations, but for an acknowledgement, perhaps even a negative one – she was, after all, now in charge of routing all incoming and outgoing communications – so, for later, she was prepared for the worst.

But the caller seemed hesitant.

Picking up the long slender piece of wood with the tiny hand at one end, a gift from a mentor, which she kept on her desk, she said: "How can I help you?" and proceeded to slowly scratch her own back.

from Marriage Lifespan Volume 6 – August 2022

Nothing to Prove

We didn´t want it. We wanted to "live in sin". So, we did for twelve years after G. moved in that first night. He had to. I had fallen out of a window – well, not a window but through the back of a bus shelter – it was cold, and I leaned in and there was no glass and I fell and cracked my head. So of course, my blind date had to take me home and stay by me in case something happened. That was in Vienna. He was, still is, Viennese.

When I got a job in Geneva, I said come along. Your turn to be a foreigner.

You´re a foreigner, too, he said.

I´m used to it. This´ll be your first time.

Twelve years later we decided to have a go at having a child. The clock was ticking, but we weren´t desperate.

On a trip back to Sydney, I told my parents about our plans. Dad was a golfer. He took my man down the back and showed him the driver. Hit him in the balls. Didn´t mean to. Sorry. Got my man hooked though. On golf.

We should get married, I said, back in Geneva. The bit of paper thing is our problem. Not the kid´s. The kid´ll have enough problems in a foreign country with foreign parents from different countries, not even a language to call their own, expressing themselves in a trilingual mish-mash. We called it communicating.

In Geneva you had to announce to the world that you were getting married. The banns or you were banned. No way.

We were going to the US anyway – an unlimited mileage holiday with the best friend who had brought us together. All over. Even Las Vegas. Not a chapel! If it rains, no go. If we fight, no go. We never fight. Always a first time. Why? Why not? Everyone does. No rings. Had to listen to the JP´s trip down the Rhine. 25$. We caught Kris Kristofferson for double that and toasted our best man with Tequila Sunrise.

The next year I was sent by my employer to a conference in Rio. My man was recovering from a knee operation. I´ll get us some rings, I said. I wanted ones that would fit his and hers, and his should look ok with hairs on the fingers. At H. Stern´s in the hotel lobby, I saw a guy with his hands, asked him what sort of ring he would wear. A coiled one was cool. I got them.

A colleague was going back to Geneva. Please pop this into our letterbox. My husband's wedding ring.

We´ve always forgotten to celebrate anniversaries. How many is it now? I made a mnemonic. 6781. We don´t wear the rings anymore, haven´t for years; the kid´s now knocking 40. This marriage so far has been one cool ride.

He golfs, cooks, shops. I wash up and write. Maybe that´s the recipe? Nothing to prove.

from Home Lifespan, Volume 7

Home Sweet Home

Where do people who don't belong go to die?
You look like us, but you don't sound like us, they said to her at school.
Why don't you go home? You don't belong.
But I want to be-long.
At the end of school, she returned to the land of her birth.
You look like us, but you don't sound like us, they said to her at uni.
Why don't you go home? You don't belong.
Not yet, she said. I want to be-long.
Write it down. Write it down.
You don't write like us, their rejections sang.
Why don't you go home? You don't belong.
So she went home to a place that was burning. People locked their doors. Through the stench of burnt koala hide, she could smell something was very wrong in the Land of Oz.
How dare you criticize the best country in the world? said a recently returned friend from a lifetime abroad.
Her friend belonged. Both here and there.
But she did not and so they fell out.
What is home? Where is home?
Where you hang your hat?
Where you hang your heart?
Where your art is?
Where your arse is?
So many questions that leave you stuck with the only one left.
To which your answer still is – not today, followed by a four-letter word. **** sweet home.

from Achievement Lifespan Volume 8

Tongue Poking

"That's quite an achievement," I say as my husband pokes out his tongue. I poke out mine and hope he will do likewise. Tongue poking is one of the logopedic exercises he should do ten times a day to be able to speak again. 120

days in ICU have caused his muscles to atrophy, but he can still blow kisses of sorts as an "I love you."

The doctor told him what would happen. No more assisted breathing. He will feel no pain. I hold his hand as the morphine kicks in. He looks straight through me.

"He can't see you, but he can hear, smell, and feel you," the palliative nurse says in answer to my unspoken question. I squeeze his hand as his breathing slows. I watch the numbers on the screen above his head. Then, in that last final flurry, he blows a kiss and pokes out his tongue."

from Loss Lifespan Volume 9

Turn, turn, turn

1. Your parents gather their small family and emigrate to the Antipodes because Australia doesn't sound too different to Austria. But it was and still is.

2. At the age of reason, you reason, you leave on a ship to see your birthland. You study, work and fall in love. That love takes you where it will: north, south, east and west.

3. You marry for $25 in Vegas, now speaking German, and in Geneva a daughter is born. *Bon Courage!* you say as she leaves for Australia. Not so different, she says. But it is.

4. She marries in Sydney and the decision is made to join her when your Austrian partner of 51 years passes away.
5. Home is where the heart is people tell you, but what if it's broken?

6. All that remains is to pick up the pieces and carry on, no longer here but there.

from Retirement Lifespan Volume 10

Gotta Keep on Rolling

I originally retired at 55 from my day job in Geneva and moved to Vienna, but it was too soon to stop working, so I got a job teaching English. Then I got a job as an editorial assistant at Vienna University, so it looked like I was going up in the world. This was after I got my PhD in Creative Writing from UNSW in 2009.

When I hit 70, I retired again, but kept on writing and published my debut novel, *All the Beautiful Liars*, in 2020 with Eye Books in the UK.

If I look at the word "retirement", it means for me getting new tires to keep on rolling. I´m just getting my goals for 2024 together, and they include reading Dostoevsky´s *The Brothers Karamazov* so that I can write a book of brothers – my father and his two brothers. Then there´s *Sensually Simmering*, a cookbook to steam the senses, and a novel, *Uncle Fritz´s Cabinet*, based on my novella in flash of the same name. So, I´ve got my work cut out for me and will need new tyres to get me there. Onwards!

from Older Lifespan Volume 11 – May 2024

In Memorium, Iris Apfel 1921-2024

When the aches tweak and I feel wobbly as the tablets multiply, I think of a teenager who made it to 102 and I get out my shocking pink sox and team them with my purple Skechers and a bright green cardigan – it's the first day of Autumn, after all – my new earrings, chunky rings and bangles and I tip my red sombrero to Iris for showing the way in her bug-eyed glasses that "more is more and less is a bore".

"If you're lucky enough to get old," she said, "celebrate it!" So I´m off to choose an appropriate nail polish – green or purple? Or gold? – before going into town for a dozen Sydney Rock Oysters and some bubbly while the sun is still shining. Rain isn't forecast…yet. And if it does rain, I have my musical psychedelic umbrella. Oh, the nailpolish – I finally opted for bright lavender vibes!

from Death Lifespan Volume 12

My Darling Dead Ones

We were three generations – my mother, my daughter and I – sitting on the front patio about to raise our brandy glasses to Dad when the bible bashers approached. Before they could start their litany, I said: "Please leave us alone. We´ve just buried my father in the garden and are bidding him farewell." Shocked, they turned and left.

When Mum died, my daughter and I dug up some of Dad´s earth/ash mix and put it in a plastic bag with Mum's ashes. We went down the bush, snipped a corner of the bag and went on their usual walk, the Mum/Dad ash mix dribbling out along the way. When the bag was empty, we'd arrived, and a kookaburra laughed.

When my husband died, we had his ashes shipped home to Australia. I´ll probably scatter them at sea near his favourite beach. He will always be near for I´ve had his wedding ring made smaller and now wear his and mine close together on my left hand, on my right is a ring Dad once gave Mum which she wore all the time after he passed.

Flash Fiction in Cow Pure Slush Vol. 23 – June 2022

A Fable

In a land nestled in mountains garden gnomes delighted in their pots of gold while lilac cows gambolled in the lush foothills. It was a land of white sheep with thick fleeces.

One day, the gnomes told the sheep stories of bedraggled others, keen to graze on their well-tended lawns.

Seized by fear, the white sheep huddled together, and conferred.

Banners then furled throughout the land: What will become of our pots of gold? Where will our sweet lilac cows now graze? Our lambs need protection. Our fleeces are pure. No to the jet-black or long-haired brown sheep.

The white sheep considered and bleated approval of far-reaching actions.

And so, what was once a rich land of beauty shrivelled to that of an insular state. The lilac cows lost their sweetness, and the white sheep became unable to lamb. All that remained were old garden gnomes hording their pots of tarnished gold.

Flash fiction in Pure Slush Music Folio 1 – Snatches of an Aria - October 2022

Battling the Heights

Anna the famous Russian opera singer with the Austrian passport – one of the few to be allowed dual nationality – spent the heatwave days in the Austrian Alps. COVID had seen to it that she wasn't the fittest, so hikes in the mountains were prescribed – also to cope with the effects of the heatwave, and to practice her latest aria.

"Up here you can practice your Puccini aria," her manager said. But Anna, although at the pinnacle of her career, was afraid of heights. So, when she and her entourage made it up the mountain and looked down, her head spun; to steady herself she took a deep breath against a rising feeling of nausea, as snatches of *O mio babbino caro/ Oh my dear Papa*

My love for which I suffer,
At last, I want to die!
Father, I beg, I beg!

were drowned out by the faster coda of a famous Neapolitan song composed for the creation of a cable railway on Mt Vesuvius.

Let's go, let's go! To the top we'll go!
Funicular up, funicular down, funicular up, funicular down!
To the top we'll go,

Funiculì, Funiculà!

Anna remembered that the funicular was later destroyed by the eruption of Vesuvius in 1944, and so knew that the popular song and not the aria was trying to tell her something.

Flash fiction in Pure Slush Music Folio 2 – Stella's Secret Sonata – June 2023

Down in the brewery

Hi, I'm Dudley Donegal O'Day, or Dud for short. I conduct, cook, collect recipes. I even planned to publish a recipe book and the book may yet see the light O'day, but not in the usual way.

I love cooking so much that I even ran a ristorante in Florence for almost ten years. My dishes were well received, but there was one problem: the patrons always wanted wine with their meal.

And I hate wine! I may even be allergic to it as it steals my voice. I'm a beer man through and through.

So, I decided to nip off to Belgium – unchronicled, of course – to a place called Leuven where the local brewery had given the populace a new type of beer. I could already feel that secret Leuven was my kind of place. I tried the beer with all my dishes. They brew it as a pilsner with just malted barley and maize, water, yeast, and noble hops. It was a clear golden straw colour with a foamy white head, which kept a decent amount of lacing when it was poured. I couldn't get enough of the light, crisp, and slightly floral taste. That night, I kept dreaming of a shapely bottle gallivanting with my dishes. In my dream, there were lots of cooks trying out their own recipes that married so well with that beer. Just like my homemade guacamole did.

I had to compose my thanks to Stella! Stella Artois, the brewery making room online for cooks and their recipes. A real star! So, I did it my way.

Flash fiction in Pure Slush Music Folio 3 – Bolero at Breakfast – February 2024

I can´t have too many Boleros

I´m penciling in 17 January 2024 at **Philharmonie Berlin**, Herbert-von-Karajan-Str. 1. If I can´t make it from Vienna to Berlin on that day, I´ll tune in to **Breakfast with Brendalee (hope she´ll still be going strong at WVOC 91.3FM**, playing *Boléro* by <u>Maurice Ravel</u>.) Because of the six-hour time difference between Vermont USA and Vienna, Austria (although the internet time zone thingy did keep looking for Vienna, USA and said they were on the same line), it´ll be well into the witching hours here in Vienna, Austria.

I fell in love with Herbert Ritter von Karajan – Ritter – he was a knight you know, when I found out that he never looked at his orchestra while conducting – a blind conductor, so to say. The Austrians abolished knighthoods and the like but were still proud of him. He passed away 34 years ago, and his widow published her autobiography, *My life by his Side* for his 100th birthday in 2008. Brendalee's programme this year with his rendering of *Bolero* brought back lots of memories that I hope to revisit next year in Berlin.

Flash fiction in Pure Slush Music Folio 4 – The Absent Bassoonist – November 2024

Just Cruising

Solomon Schweitzer was a bit of a computer nerd and was always experimenting how to get more fans of his bassoon. His cosplay mates wanted him to play for them on the Jo Co Cruise, a week-long event at sea with music, panels and comedy. So Solomon had to choose between the cruise and the *Bassoon Concerto*. And he did. But he didn´t tell the organizers of the *Bassoon Concerto*, for fear they would not approve.

What I am left wondering, dear audience, is will our First Bassoonist grace us with his presence tonight?" Maestro sighs. "And if not, where on this blessed earth is he?!"

"He's on a cruise," a voice pipes up from the back of the room.

"A cruise?"

"Not any old cruise. The Jo Co Cruise. They needed a bassoonist for the musical performance! And you know what a nerd Solomon is. He couldn´t say no."

Flash fiction in World Literature Today – September 2012

BAKU

I am an old man. I am invisible, almost as invisible as my sister. My sister lives in the house of her husband near the sea, in the house of his father and his fathers before him. My sister is younger, younger than I am, but not too young to have forgotten Black January. For the sake of her daughters, she has screened it out. Her daughters, my nieces, they are our spring.

Lights flash in colours of red, white, blue, green and her daughters sing words unknown to me: oh oh-uh-oh oh, woki po-po. They sing of love and they hum. They were down by the water bathing in light streams when bulldozer men came to the house. Men with mallets did not see their mother, for, as I said, she was invisible. She did not sing. Nor did she hum.

When her husband came home her daughters were still bathing in glowlights and singing strange words. In the rubble, he screamed; a young child called out, 'Freedom'. The police came, took the young child away. Him, they left crumpled and broken where once stood the house, that of his father and his fathers before him.

On the television, babushki, no longer invisible, sing of parties to cheering crowds. Down in the streets young people sing freedom. Policemen come, lights flash their colours; the police leave the young people alone.

I think of my sister. Did they not see her because she did not sing? My nieces are beautiful in red, white, blue, green. I think of their father with no house to live in. Will the colours still flash when the singing stops? I put down the telephone, turn off the television. I am too old to learn another new song.

Essays in World Literature Today

Meeting Friederike Mayröcker (1924-2021): A Remembrance, July 13, 2021

Friederike Mayröcker reading, not long after the Book-themed TV Series Über featured her in its first episode

Friederike Mayröcker passed away on June 4, 2021, in Vienna, aged ninety-six. She was farewelled to Louis Armstrong's "What a Wonderful World" and was laid to rest on June 17 in a grave of honor at the Central Cemetery beside her partner of many years, the poet Ernst Jandl, who died in 2000. I was fortunate to meet Mayröcker, albeit in a roundabout way.

I was involved with editing an anthology of prose, poetry, and artwork called New Sun Rising: Stories for Japan to raise money for the Japanese Red Cross following the Fukushima earthquake in 2011. I had gone to the Literaturhaus to see Marion Steinfellner, a Viennese poet and Butoh dancer. When I mentioned the anthology, she immediately said that Mayröcker had written a poem mentioning Japanese cats that might fit the anthology, and that I needed to meet her confidante, Christel Fallenstein, who would be able to guide me.

Christel Fallenstein was very helpful; Mayröcker agreed to participate and donated the poem, but it had to be rendered in English. The translator Liselotte Pope-Hofmann, who had already translated some of Mayröcker's work, agreed to translate the poem, the pertinent parts of which are:

... while the Japanese cats namely the cats are weeping actually waving: wailing you know nothing matters ...

... as for the eye-slits of the cats which in the ZONE = forbidden zone are wandering about and weeping and crying ...

We were finalizing the anthology, but I felt Mayröcker's poem would make a good link between the introduction and the works themselves donated by artists and writers from all over the world.

In 2014 the 13th International Conference on the Short Story in English was held in Vienna. As Vienna co-director, I was responsible for ensuring that we also had good local representation. Again, I thought how great it would be to have Mayröcker read in a plenary session in German and have the English translation scroll behind her on a large screen.

"But I do not write short stories," she said.

"Ah, but the form is changing," I said, "there are so many ways to tell a story. Just look at Empress Sissi, how her hair curls in tendrils escaping every which way. This, too, is story."

We already had discussed the first flash fictions two years earlier at the 12th International Conference in North Little Rock.

Liselotte Pope-Hofmann agreed once more to translate Mayröcker, this time for the Vienna conference, which welcomed short-story writers from around the world. One of these was the Australian short-story writer and poet Andy Kissane, who immediately hit it off with Mayröcker and gave her one of his own poetry books and just sent me these words: "I met Friederike Mayröcker at the International Conference on the Short Story in English in Vienna in 2014. We read at an Austrian/Australian event together at Alte Schmiede and I caught up with her afterwards at the conference. My father was about her age at the time, and was running a choir in the aged care home where he lived, and we talked about that and how she was writing every day. She was warm, welcoming, and so full of energy for poetry and for life."

Two poets, attending a short-story conference, helped everyone appreciate the changing short-story genre. Just the year before, American writer Lydia Davis had won the Man Booker for her very short fiction, setting the stage for an explosion of the short form in what is today practiced as flash fiction.

On one wonderful evening, Austrian and Australian writers attending the conference read from their works in their own language in the Alte Schmiede.

We issued a limited edition of stories by Austrian and Australian writers in German with an introduction by the Australian ambassador. Sales of the anthology went toward financing the participation of one of the Austrian writers, Judith Nika Pfeifer, at the next Short Story Conference in Shanghai two years later.

After the conference, I met up several times with Mayröcker, by chance and at readings, the latter from her 2016 book *Fleurs*, which contained a poem revised on April 13, 2014, which, to my great delight and honor, she signed for me. I recognized our discussion and how I tried to convince her to attend a "short-story conference."

> your suggestion, my slim writings = these hallucinatory pieces of poetry
> ought
> to be called "short stories", makes me marvel,
>
> I am holding my hands in front of my face how
> I am crying. In my little room,
> facing s/w, lop-sided typewriting desk "hermes
> baby" with piano music by
> Franz sacred morning hour. Outside
> spring end of March I can see
> that the lilac is thriving, at times
> I copy from my dreams,
> I receive verbaldreams. I sit bent over
> almost kneeling (like Glenn Gould
> playing like possessed), one needs to be able
> to wait until it clicks, I
> need a high room temperature and
> electric light even when the
> sun is shining in. It is a great
> excitement so that my
> blood pressure level in the highest, etc. Am
> full of courage and thank the Holy
> Ghost for his promises . . .

new version, April 13, 2014, © by FM
Translation by Liselotte Pope-Hoffmann

When *Fleurs* was published by Suhrkamp in 2016, I was thrilled to find the original of the above and of course asked to have the page signed.

»dein Vorschlag, meine schmalen Schriften = diese halluzinatorischen
Stücke von Poesie als »Kurzgeschichten« zu bezeichnen, nimmt
mich wunder, ich halte mir die Hände vors Gesicht wie ich weine.
In meinem Kämmerchen, SW-Seite, schiefer Maschinenschreibtisch,
»hermes baby« zu Klaviermusik von Franz Liszt heilige Morgenstunde.
Drauszen Frühling Ende März ich sehe dasz der Flieder sprieszt,
manchmal schreibe ich von meinen Träumen ab, ich empfange
Verbalträume. Ich sitze gebückt fast kniend (wie Glenn Gould beim
rasenden Spiel), man musz warten können bis es einschnappt, ich
brauche eine hohe Zimmertemperatur und elektrisches Licht auch
wenn die Sonne hereinscheint. Es ist eine grosze Aufregung so dasz
mein Blutdruckwert aufs höchste, etc. Bin sehr beherzt und danke
dem heiligen Geist für seine Verheiszungen ....«

neue Version am 13.4.14

für Sylvia

It was no surprise to see a visit to Mayröcker—always one to be interested
in what younger writers were up to—kick off the new book TV series ÜBER,
created by Judith Nika Pfeifer and Daniela Emminger in 2020. Their aim is to
make books and reading "cool" again and every couple of months to introduce
an author and related works. At 07:57 in the first episode of ÜBER, you can
see them visit Mayröcker just before her ninety-sixth birthday last year.

She will be missed by young and old, but her words will live on. I am so
proud and moved to have been able to meet her.

Home in the Face of Grief, March 13, 2024

A writer considers home as she remembers her partner
of fifty-one years.

I was born in Vienna and grew up in Australia. We didn't speak German at home. My parents were "new" Australians for whom migration meant one country, one nationality. Australia.

My generation was a lucky one, with perhaps a short memory. Uni was free with a Commonwealth scholarship as the last year of the five-year high school system. I left Sydney straight after finishing my exams in French, German, and psychology. Not for a gap year. I wanted to see where I was born. Vienna. And after that, no plans.

Professor Hesse, my German professor at University of New South Wales, also a "new" Australian who had transited via a university career in then-apartheid South Africa, taught me that education wasn't about marks and degrees.

He encouraged me to go to literary events, and at one, I met the Austrian poet Rudi Krausmann (1933–2019), who gave me a story by Heinrich Böll, "Die ungezählte Geliebte." In English, it's called "At the Bridge."

It's about a war veteran whose job is to count how many people cross a bridge. He secretly falls in love with a girl and does not include her in his statistics. When he gazes after her, others also slip through. I kept the photocopy of the story in my papers for years. Forgotten.

But I recently found it again, and I think the not-being-counted represents how I found my voice and perhaps my identity.

I've been going through all the bits of paper and knickknacks collected over the space of a life. Not just mine.

I've been going through all the bits of paper and knickknacks collected over the space of a life. Not just mine.

Günter, my husband and partner of fifty-one years, passed away last May, attacked by necrotizing pancreatitis and left to waste in the ICU for four months. It was nobody's fault. Just one of those things. May he rest in peace. Peace was what he wanted.

We met in Vienna, his hometown, in the 1970s. I'd just arrived from Australia to see the city where I'd been born. I'd grown up in Sydney and wanted to study translation at the University of Vienna. He said he was an *installateur* (plumber). I, declining a verb as a way out of my incomprehension, asked, *"Was installen Sie?"* (What do you install?). We both had to laugh, sealing our fate.

It was autumn, and our first date was a stroll in the central cemetery to watch the squirrels look for food to hoard against winter.

Where do people who don't belong go to die?

I had begun to have flashes about belonging. Some came from the past, some from the present.

At school they said: "You look like us, but you don't sound like us. Why don't you go home? You don't belong."

But I want to be-long.

At the end of uni in Sydney, I returned to the land of my birth.

At uni in Vienna, where I was studying translation, they said: "You look like us, but you don't sound like us. Why don't you go home?"

You don't belong.

Not yet, I said. I want to be-long.

Write It Down. Write It Down

It's all grist for the mill, voices said, albeit small ones in my head.

"You don't write like us," their rejections sang.

"Why don't you go home? You don't belong."

So I went home to a place that was burning. People locked their doors. Through the stench of burnt koala hide, I could smell something was very wrong in the Land of Oz.

"How dare you criticize the best country in the world?" a recently returned friend from a lifetime abroad said. My friend belonged. Both here and there.

But I did not and so we fell out.

What is home? Where is home?

Where your heart is?

Where your art is?

Where your arse is?

So many questions that leave you stuck with the only one left.

Where do people who don't belong go to die?

A Flushed Flash

An Egyptian friend sent as a condolence: "We live and remember."

Our daughter went alone to collect the ashes.

We had to have a paper from the embassy saying it was okay to take them to Australia. The paper came by email.

The Austrians didn't like the idea of scatterable ashes being handed over just like that. Here they were placed in urns and buried in family graves so that family members could continue arguing for all eternity.

He wouldn't have wanted that. We would scatter his ashes on his favorite golf course—Turramurra—a chopper course, he called it. It surely wouldn't mind his ashes.

But we weren't going till next year. Going forever.

"Put them under the stairs," I said. They were in a shiny round tin in a plain brown cardboard box. It just fit.

On the wall above the stairs, there are photos of times of our lives, fifty-one years of fun and love. I see them from my bed next to the one missing his body.

"We mustn't forget them," I said.

"We won't," said my daughter. "The jewelry's there."

We laughed. He would have, too. Then we cried.

I waited for grief, but it didn't come. So, I wrote flashes. I couldn't bear more.

Two got published in Australia's Pure Slush's Lifespan Series entitled *Achievement and Loss*. Pure Slush had already brought my flashes on work (Volume 5), marriage (Volume 6), and home (Volume 7). It was a little like coming home to have my flashes accepted there.

Achievement (volume 8) and *Loss* (volume 9) were closer to the bone as I tried to come to terms with my grief but did not want to wallow.

I was going to post those two flashes here, but they left in boxes to be sea-freighted to Australia when possible, and are now in the eighty-five-box cargo sitting in Brno awaiting delivery to a Dutch port from whence they will sail to the Land of Oz. Am I going home? To where I be-long? I found the flash I had written and submitted to *Achievement* on my hard drive. I can't seem to find the flash entitled *Loss*. Maybe it's too early.

Beginnings

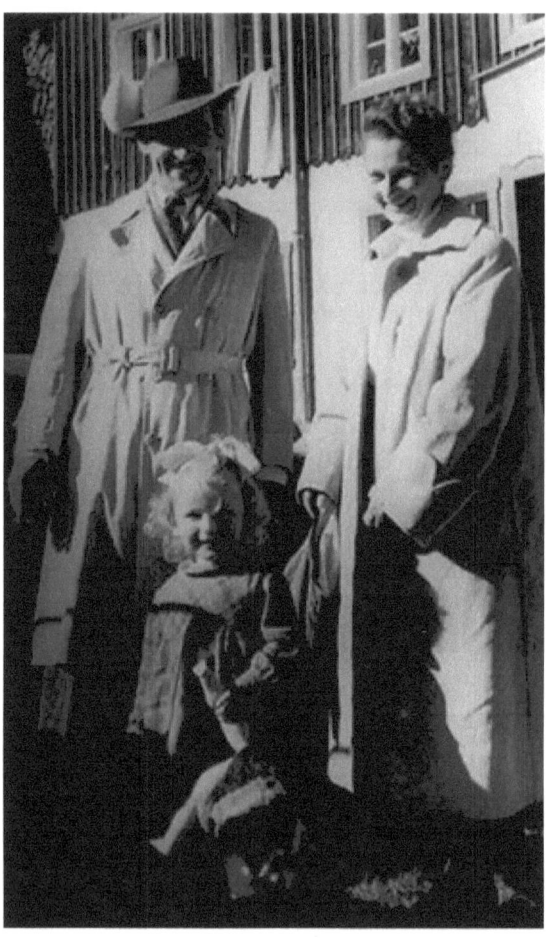

My parents immigrated to Australia with me when I was about three.

I left for Vienna when I was twenty to see my birthplace, find my roots. There I found my rock, the man I've been with for fifty-one years. The man who was also going to come to Australia. It was not to be.

My jobs took us to Helsinki, Brussels, Geneva, and then through conferences to Brazil, Argentina, Istanbul, and more. We married in Las Vegas for twenty-five dollars, honeymooned on a yacht in the Virgin Islands. Our daughter was born in Geneva and took off for Sydney to study.

Maarit and Günter

Now she is with me in Vienna, sharing my grief, packing boxes for the move back to Sydney. Only the minimum. Just things that matter and are close to our hearts like papers and photos and paintings, and books.

My husband had a Driza-Bone, which I gave to a young Australian friend in Vienna. Here is Günter, in his Driza-Bone, enjoying a glass with Karli, an Austrian friend, married to a French woman and based in Switzerland where we also lived.

I could break it all down into slices of twenty, twenty years per slice: Sydney—Vienna—Geneva—Vienna—Sydney. Four were homes; he was with me for three.

So, going back to the question, Where is home?

I guess it must be where your heart is/was, would have been. Günter and I were going to get so old together; we both even quit smoking a good while ago.

Home will soon be Sydney again. I will nurse my grief, look at old photos, talk to my husband and thank him for the half-century we explored life and the world together. He was loved by young and old. He even danced rock 'n' roll in an Austrian kilt at our daughter Sydney's wedding.

It's good that I'm going back to Sydney. I would be too lonely in Vienna. My daughter and her husband can put me up in the spare room of their flat until we find a house with a yard where I can have a granny flat built—a two-bedder so as to have a room for visitors.

I will have pots and plants and bookshelves. I will join the local library to keep costs down. I will become a minimalist, an independent one, not falling

Dancing in 2015

on anyone's turf. My own woman, *quoi*! Maybe then, words will pour out of me, helping me to overcome my grief.

The stories will decide what they are to be about. I shall experiment, venture into the realm of crime—romance I need to leave aside for a while.

As the pendulum swings to the right in Europe, I'm a bit worried about what awaits me in the Land of Oz.

A new chapter—that's the only way I can move on. I can start a new and exciting chapter and still go back and read what came before. I can also look ahead and see where life takes me in this last segment of my life. I can tell him all about it, spin tales to keep him close. I'll put on some music. He liked Rod Stewart—maybe there's a kilt-link there.

He didn't have a funeral. We invited friends to come by in July and bid him farewell, the way he would have liked. They came from far and wide— Helsinki, Geneva, Vienna. His birthday was at the close of November, so our daughter cooked his favorite meal—meatloaf and mashed potatoes with a colonel for dessert (lemon sorbet with a shot of vodka). We were three at table—our daughter, Maarit; our lodger, Günther; and me. My Günter would have enjoyed it.

This will be the first Christmas without him. We have lots to do as we empty the house pending a sale. Yesterday, men came to pick up eighty-five boxes.

Things here are coming to an end. It may be a sign. Like my dry skin flaking off, making space for a renewal that will always hold him dear. I can hear him nodding.

Things here are coming to an end. It may be a sign.

It's been a great ride all around the world and more. Those eighty-five boxes contain treasures that will come alive when we meet up with them in Sydney. Their contents will link to memories that will sustain me in the new chapter of my life.

Vale Günter Linsbauer: lover, husband, father of our wonderful Maarit, and as a friend said, gentle giant with a big heart. It's been a pleasure and an honor to have shared the ride with you.

"What do you install?" I asked many years ago. A life well lived, a love well loved, are the answers that now come forth despite having been too short. I recall the Egyptian condolence I received, now so apt: "We live and remember."

I hope I can do all the memories justice when I go "home," where "home" is no longer a place, but a state of mind that will have to sustain me for at least twenty more years, for I have stories to write.

— Vienna / Sydney

www.ingramcontent.com/pod-product-compliance
Lightning Source LLC
Chambersburg PA
CBHW060404030726
47497CB00003B/844